SOMETIMES WHEN IT RAINS

Sometimes when it rains
I smile to myself
And think of times when as a child
I'd sit by myself
And wonder why people need clothes

Sometimes when it rains
I think of times
when I'd run into the rain
Shouting 'Nkce – nkce mlanjana
When will I grow?
I'll grow up tomorrow!'

Sometimes when it rains
I think of times
When I watched goats
running so fast from the rain
While sheep seemed to enjoy it

Sometimes when it rains
I think of times
When we had to undress
Carry the small bundles of uniforms and books
On our heads
And cross the river after school

Sometimes when it rains
I remember times
When it would rain hard for hours
And fill our drum
so we didn't have to fetch water
From the river for a day or two

SOMETIMES WHEN IT RAINS

Sometimes when it rains
Rains for many hours without break
I think of people
who have nowhere to go
No home of their own
And no food to eat
Only rain water to drink

Sometimes when it rains
Rains for days without break
I think of mothers
Who give birth in squatter camps
Under plastic shelters
At the mercy of cold angry winds

Sometimes when it rains
I think of 'illegal' job seekers
in big cities
Dodging police vans in the rain
Hoping for darkness to come
So they can find some wet corner to hide in

Sometimes when it rains
Rains so hard hail joins in
I think of life prisoners
in all the jails of the world
And wonder if they still love
To see the rainbow at the end of the rain

Sometimes when it rains
With hail stones biting the grass
I can't help thinking they look like teeth
Many teeth of smiling friends
Then I wish that everyone else
Had something to smile about.

Gcina Mhlope

SOMETIMES
WHEN IT RAINS

PANDORA PRESS FICTION

SOMETIMES WHEN IT RAINS

WRITINGS BY SOUTH AFRICAN WOMEN

Edited by Ann Oosthuizen

Linocuts by Bongiwe Dhlomo

PANDORA

London and New York

This collection first published in 1987 by
Pandora Press (Routledge & Kegan Paul Ltd)
11 New Fetter Lane, London EC4P 4EE

Published in the USA by
Pandora Press (Routledge & Kegan Paul Inc.)
in association with Methuen Inc.
29 West 35th Street, New York, NY 10001

Set in 10/11pt. Sabon
by Columns of Reading
and printed in Great Britain
by The Guernsey Press Co Ltd
Guernsey, Channel Islands

Library of Congress Cataloging in Publication Data
Sometimes when it rains.
1. Short stories, South African (English) –
Women authors.   2. South Africa – History –
1961-   – Fiction.   3. Women – Fiction.
I. Oosthuizen, Ann.
PR9367.33.W65S66   1987   823'.01'089287   86-25490
British Library CIP Data also available
ISBN 0-86358-107-2(c)
      0-86358-198-6 (ppr)

316702

*T*here is an intense need for self-expression among the oppressed in our country. When I say self-expression I don't mean people saying something about themselves. I mean people making history consciously.... We neglect the creativity that has made the people able to survive extreme exploitation and oppression. People have survived extreme racism. It means our people have been creative about their lives.

Mongane Serote, *Staffrider*, vol. 4, no. 1, Ravan Press, April/May 1981

CONTENTS

CONTENTS

ILLUSTRATIONS

by Bongiwe Dhlomo

EDITOR'S INTRODUCTION

Imagine that you are travelling through South Africa. On your journey you are fortunate to meet and talk with fourteen women. One of them is an artist. Several are outstanding writers. Some stories are imagined, others keep closer to events in the writer's life, or transcribe an interview with a great, or an ordinary woman.

You may not agree with everything you hear. Some stories may make uncomfortable reading. You are travelling through a violent society in the grip of change and chaos. Those who write about it are not always able to stand back and take a larger view, and often the writer may not be talking to you in her own language.

Lunching with one of the writers in a mid-town restaurant in Johannesburg, I remarked at how difficult it was for me to reconcile the scene around us with the war that was taking place in the townships which encircle the city.

'Yes,' she answered. 'When I drive home after work, when I leave the motorway, it's as if I'm in an entirely different place.'

'Don't you feel angry?'

'I think if I let myself feel anger, there'd be no stopping it; I'd go mad.'

There is a generosity in these stories that is, I believe, part of the greatness of Africa. They do not treat the reader as a stranger. Whatever their colour, the authors write about families and communities that have been mutilated by apartheid. They write about being made to work as servants for families not their own, about the migrant labour system. This is the core of women's experience. By asserting this reality, they collapse the boundaries between rich and poor, black and white. They have not only changed the way I regard those who are not of my race and class, they have given me something new, for myself. Something of their courage, and strength, and pride, has been transferred to me. I smile, and am glad to be alive in the same world.

Ann Oosthuizen

THE TOILET

Gcina Mhlope

Sometimes I wanted to give up and be a good girl who listened to her elders. Maybe I should have done something like teaching or nursing as my mother wished. People thought these professions were respectable, but I knew I wanted to do something different, though I was not sure what. I thought a lot about acting. . . . My mother said that it had been a waste of good money educating me because I did not know what to do with the knowledge I had acquired. I'd come to Johannesburg for the December holidays after writing my matric exams, and then stayed on, hoping to find something to do.

My elder sister worked in Orange Grove as a domestic worker, and I stayed with her in her back room. I didn't know anybody in Jo'burg except my sister's friends whom we went to church with. The Methodist church up Fourteenth Avenue was about the only outing we had together. I was very bored and lonely.

On weekdays I was locked in my sister's room so that the Madam wouldn't see me. She was at home most of the time: painting her nails, having tea with her friends, or lying in the sun by the swimming pool. The swimming pool was very close to the room, which is why I had to keep very quiet. My sister felt bad about locking me in there, but she had no alternative. I couldn't even play the radio, so she brought me books, old magazines, and newspapers from the white people. I just read every single thing I came across: *Fair Lady*, *Woman's Weekly*, anything. But then my sister thought I was reading too much.

'What kind of wife will you make if you can't even make baby clothes, or knit yourself a jersey? I suppose you will marry an educated man like yourself, who won't mind going to bed with a book and an empty stomach.'

We would play cards at night when she knocked off, and listen to the radio, singing along softly with the songs we liked.

1

Then I got this temporary job in a clothing factory in town. I looked forward to meeting new people, and liked the idea of being out of that room for a change. The factory made clothes for ladies' boutiques.

The whole place was full of machines of all kinds. Some people were sewing, others were ironing with big heavy irons that pressed with a lot of steam. I had to cut all the loose threads that hang after a dress or a jacket is finished. As soon as a number of dresses in a certain style were finished, they would be sent to me and I had to count them, write the number down, and then start with the cutting of the threads. I was fascinated to discover that one person made only sleeves, another the collars, and so on until the last lady put all the pieces together, sewed on buttons, or whatever was necessary to finish.

Most people at the factory spoke Sotho, but they were nice to me – they tried to speak to me in Zulu or Xhosa, and they gave me all kinds of advice on things I didn't know. There was this girl, Gwendolene – she thought I was very stupid – she called me a 'bari' because I always sat inside the changing room with something to read when it was time to eat my lunch, instead of going outside to meet guys. She told me it was cheaper to get myself a 'lunch boy' – somebody to buy me lunch. She told me it was wise not to sleep with him, because then I could dump him anytime I wanted to. I was very nervous about such things. I thought it was better to be a 'bari' than to be stabbed by a city boy for his money.

The factory knocked off at four-thirty, and then I went to a park near where my sister worked. I waited there till half past six, when I could sneak into the house again without the white people seeing me. I had to leave the house before half past five in the mornings as well. That meant I had to find something to do with the time I had before I could catch the seven-thirty bus to work – about two hours. I would go to a public toilet in the park. For some reason it was never locked, so I would go in and sit on the toilet seat to read some magazine or other until the right time to catch the bus.

The first time I went into this toilet, I was on my way to the bus stop. Usually I went straight to the bus stop outside the OK Bazaars where it was well lit, and I could see. I would wait there, reading, or just looking at the growing number of cars and buses on their way to town. On this day it was raining quite hard, so I thought I would shelter in the toilet until the rain had passed. I knocked first to see if there was anyone inside. As there was no reply, I pushed the door open and went in. It smelled a little – a dryish kind of smell, as if the toilet was not used all that often, but it was quite clean compared to many 'Non-European' toilets I knew. The floor was painted red and the walls were cream white. It did not look like it had been painted for a few years. I stood looking around, with the rain coming very hard on the zinc roof. The noise was comforting – to know I had escaped the wet – only a few of the heavy drops had got me. The plastic bag in which I carried my book and purse and neatly folded pink handkerchief was a little damp, but that was because I had used it to cover my head when I ran to the toilet. I pulled my dress down a little so that it would not get creased when I sat down. The closed lid of the toilet was going to be my seat for many mornings after that.

I was really lucky to have found that toilet because the winter was very cold. Not that it was any warmer in there, but once I'd closed the door it used to be a little less windy. Also the toilet was very small – the walls were wonderfully close to me – it felt like it was made to fit me alone. I enjoyed that kind of privacy. I did a lot of thinking while I sat on that toilet seat. I did a lot of daydreaming too – many times imagining myself in some big hall doing a really popular play with other young actors. At school, we took set books like *Buzani KuBawo* or *A Man for All Seasons* and made school plays which we toured to the other schools on weekends. I loved it very much. When I was even younger I had done little sketches taken from the Bible and on big days like Good Friday, we acted and sang happily.

I would sit there dreaming. . . .

I was getting bored with the books I was reading – the love stories all sounded the same, and besides that I just lost interest. I started asking myself why I had not written anything since I left school. At least at school I had written some poems, or stories for the school magazine, school competitions and other magazines like *Bona* and *Inkqubela*. Our English teacher was always so encouraging; I remembered the day I showed him my first poem – I was so excited I couldn't concentrate in class for the whole day. I didn't know anything about publishing then, and I

3

didn't ask myself if my stories were good enough. I just enjoyed writing things down when I had the time. So one Friday, after I'd started being that toilet's best customer, I bought myself a notebook in which I was hoping to write something. I didn't use it for quite a while, until one evening.

My sister had taken her usual Thursday afternoon off, and she had delayed somewhere. I came back from work, then waited in the park for the right time to go back into the yard. The white people always had their supper at six-thirty and that was the time I used to steal my way in without disturbing them or being seen. My comings and goings had to be secret because they still didn't know I stayed there.

Then I realised that she hadn't come back, and I was scared to go out again, in case something went wrong this time. I decided to sit down in front of my sister's room, where I thought I wouldn't be noticed. I was reading a copy of *Drum Magazine* and hoping that she would come back soon – before the dogs sniffed me out. For the first time I realised how stupid it was of me not to have cut myself a spare key long ago. I kept on hearing noises that sounded like the gate opening. A few times I was sure I had heard her footsteps on the concrete steps leading to the servant's quarters, but it turned out to be something or someone else.

I was trying hard to concentrate on my reading again, when I heard the two dogs playing, chasing each other nearer and nearer to where I was sitting. And then, there they were in front of me, looking as surprised as I was. For a brief moment we stared at each other, then they started to bark at me. I was sure they would tear me to pieces if I moved just one finger, so I sat very still, trying not to look at them, while my heart pounded and my mouth went dry as paper.

They barked even louder when the dogs from next door joined in, glared at me through the openings in the hedge. Then the Madam's high-pitched voice rang out above the dogs' barking.

'Ireeeeeeeene!' That's my sister's English name, which we never use. I couldn't move or answer the call – the dogs were standing right in front of me, their teeth so threateningly long. When there was no reply, she came to see what was going on.

'Oh, it's you? Hello.' She was smiling at me, chewing that gum which never left her mouth, instead of calling the dogs away

4

from me. They had stopped barking, but they hadn't moved – they were still growling at me, waiting for her to tell them what to do.

'Please Madam, the dogs will bite me,' I pleaded, not moving my eyes from them.

'No, they won't bite you.' Then she spoke to them nicely, 'Get away now – go on,' and they went off. She was like a doll, her hair almost orange in colour, all curls round her made-up face. Her eyelashes fluttered like a doll's. Her thin lips were bright red like her long nails, and she wore very high-heeled shoes. She was still smiling; I wondered if it didn't hurt after a while. When her friends came for a swim, I could always hear her forever laughing at something or other.

She scared me – I couldn't understand how she could smile like that but not want me to stay in her house.

'When did you come in? We didn't see you.'

'I've been here for some time now – my sister isn't here. I'm waiting to talk to her.'

'Oh – she's not here?' She was laughing, for no reason that I could see. 'I can give her a message – you go on home – I'll tell her that you want to see her.'

Once I was outside the gate, I didn't know what to do or where to go. I walked slowly, kicking my heels. The street lights were so very bright! Like big eyes staring at me. I wondered what the people who saw me thought I was doing, walking around at that time of the night. But then I didn't really care, because there wasn't much I could do about the situation right then. I was just thinking how things had to go wrong on that day particularly, because my sister and I were not on such good terms. Early that morning, when the alarm had gone for me to wake up, I did not jump to turn it off, so my sister got really angry with me. She had gone on about me always leaving it to ring for too long, as if it was set for her, and not for me. And when I went out to wash, I had left the door open a second too long, and that was enough to earn me another scolding.

Every morning I had to wake up straight away, roll my bedding and put it all under the bed where my sister was sleeping. I was not supposed to put on the light although it was still dark. I'd light a candle, and tiptoe my way out with a soap dish and a toothbrush. My clothes were on a hanger on a nail at

5

the back of the door. I'd take the hanger and close the door as quietly as I could. Everything had to be ready set the night before. A washing basin full of cold water was also ready outside the door, put there because the sound of running water and the loud screech the taps made in the morning could wake the white people and they would wonder what my sister was doing up so early. I'd do my everything and be off the premises by five-thirty with my shoes in my bag – I only put them on once I was safely out of the gate. And that gate made such a noise too. Many time I wished I could jump over it and save myself all that sickening careful-careful business!

Thinking about all these things took my mind away from the biting cold of the night and my wet nose, until I saw my sister walking towards me.

'Mholo, what are you doing outside in the street?' she greeted me. I quickly briefed her on what had happened.

'Oh Yehovah! You can be so dumb sometimes! What were you doing inside in the first place? You know you should have waited for me so we could walk in together. Then I could say you were visiting or something. Now, you tell me, what am I supposed to say to them if they see you come in again? Hayi!'

She walked angrily towards the gate, with me hesitantly following her. When she opened the gate, she turned to me with an impatient whisper.

'And now why don't you come in, stupid?'

I mumbled my apologies, and followed her in. By some miracle no one seemed to have noticed us, and we quickly munched a snack of cold chicken and boiled potatoes and drank our tea, hardly on speaking terms. I just wanted to howl like a dog. I wished somebody would come and be my friend, and tell me that I was not useless, and that my sister did not hate me, and tell me that one day I would have a nice place to live . . . anything. It would have been really great to have someone my own age to talk to.

But also I knew that my sister was worried for me, she was scared of her employers. If they were to find out that I lived with her, they would fire her, and then we would both be walking up and down the streets. My eleven rand wages wasn't going to help us at all. I don't know how long I lay like that, unable to fall asleep, just wishing and wishing with tears running into my ears.

The next morning I woke up long before the alarm went off, but I just lay there feeling tired and depressed. If there was a way out, I would not have gone to work, but there was this other strong feeling or longing inside me. It was some kind of pain that pushed me to do everything at double speed and run to my toilet. I call it my toilet because that is exactly how I felt about it. It was very rare that I ever saw anybody else go in there in the mornings. It was like they all knew I was using it, and they had to lay off or something. When I went there, I didn't really expect to find it occupied.

I felt my spirits really lifting as I put on my shoes outside the gate. I made sure that my notebook was in my bag. In my haste I even forgot my lunchbox, but it didn't matter I was walking faster and my feet were feeling lighter all the time. Then I noticed that the door had been painted, and that a new window pane had replaced the old broken one. I smiled to myself as I reached the door. Before long I was sitting on that toilet seat, writing a poem.

Many more mornings saw me sitting there writing. Sometimes it did not need to be a poem; I wrote anything that came into my head – in the same way I would have done if I'd had a friend to talk to. I remember some days when I felt like I was hiding something from my sister. She did not know about my toilet in the park, and she was not in the least interested in my notebook.

Then one morning I wanted to write a story about what had happened at work the day before; the supervisor screaming at me for not calling her when I'd seen the people who stole two dresses at lunch time. I had found it really funny. I had to write about it and I just hoped there were enough pages left in my notebook. It all came back to me, and I was smiling when I reached for the door, but it wouldn't open – it was locked!

I think for the first time I accepted that the toilet was not mine after all. . . . Slowly I walked over to a bench nearby, watched the early spring sun come up, and wrote my story anyway.

IT'S QUIET NOW

Gcina Mhlope

Everyone seems to be going to bed now. The rain is coming down in a steady downpour, and I don't think it's going to stop for a long time. Normally I would be joining the others, going to bed while it's still raining so that I can enjoy the sound of it while I wait for sleep to come and take me. I don't want to play any soft music either. I just want to stand here at the window and watch what can be seen of the rain coming down in the dark.

The news in the papers is always the same – some people's house petrol-bombed, youths and activists arrested, suspected informer necklaced, police shootings – it only varies from place to place. It's been like this for . . . I don't know how long. It's really depressing. Today I did not even have to buy a paper, things just kept happening since late this morning.

The PUTCO buses have not been going into the townships. Last week they started coming into our township again. The newspapers said that the local Residents' Association had gone to ask the authorities to bring back the buses, but members of the Association know nothing about it. Most old people seemed quite relieved that the buses were back, but they knew it wouldn't last. Company delivery vans have not been coming in either; the students have burnt so many of them in the past few months.

The house of the local 'Mayor' was also burnt down. It was at one o'clock after midnight when we were woken up by two loud explosions one after the other, and soon the house was eaten up by hungry flames. The 'Mayor' and his family just made it out of the house, running for their lives. Everything was burnt to ashes by the time the police and fire engines arrived. When I saw his house like that, I remembered what he had said a few weeks back in a Residents' meeting.

'You seem to forget that I am as black as you are, and I suffer

8

just like you do under the apartheid laws of this country.' The grumbling from the audience showed that nobody believed him.

A lot of things have been happening here; I just can't keep track. Young children who hardly understand what is really going on are also shouting the slogan 'Siyayinyova' which simply means 'We will destroy or disrupt'.

Nobody was expecting anything today, even though there were more policemen than usual – there have been police driving up and down our streets for quite a while now. We carry on with our work and sort of pretend they are not there.

I was carrying on with my work as well, when I suddenly heard singing. I ran to the window and there, at a school in Eighth Avenue, these children – you know I can still see them as if there's a photograph in my mind. . . . They poured out of their classes into the streets, where the police were. They were shouting 'Siyayinyova!' at the tops of their little voices. They picked up rocks and bricks and started attacking buses, company delivery vans and police cars. When the police started chasing them, they ran through double-ups (small paths cutting through people's houses). I stood transfixed at the window. There was running everywhere, just school uniforms all over the township, and shouting and chanting and screaming and burning of policemen's and councillors' houses.

Two company vans were burnt in front of the house right opposite us. The fire jumped and caught on to the house as well, and then there was black smoke from the house and the cars and the cars in the next street and the next. . . . Soon the streets were lost in the dust and smoke.

Clouds from earth began to meet clouds from the sky. We suddenly heard – *qhwara*! *qhwara*! Lighting and thunder! Louder than any bomb or gun. Poor soldiers, their guns came down as the rain began to fall – *whhhaaaaa*. . . . Maybe it came to clean up the mess.

People started coming back from work. It kept on raining and no one even ran. They walked in the rain as if everything was as they had left it. Some had heard the news from work, and others could see that a lot had happened. But they walked home as usual and got on with their suppers. I didn't have an appetite at supper. I wonder if I should go to sleep now. There is only a light drizzle coming down and all seems quiet in the night.

9

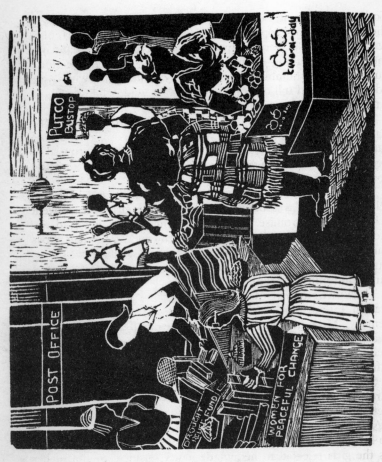

Women at work

TWO MINUTES

Maud Motanyane

Tosh and I were an odd pair; she was tall and thin, and I was short and plump. People called us the big and small twins, or B & S for short. In very many ways we were different, and yet there was something strong that bound us together. We stood out like sore thumbs from the rest of the girls, who were adventurous and full of pranks. They were wild, while Tosh and I tried to lead a life as pure as possible.

It is twenty years since I last saw Tosh, and I feel guilty that I have not been back to see her. I am sure she is plagued by the same guilt. We made a vow many years ago, and we promised to keep it whatever happened. We crossed each other's hearts and spat on the ground as we promised.

' "Strue's God, my friend, if I ever do it I will come back and tell you." There was only one 'it' that little girls in a convent school could promise not to get themselves involved in. According to Sister Marietta, the matron of the convent, boys came second after witches and ghosts as the deadliest poison for little girls. It could take less than two minutes for a boy to ruin a girl's entire life, she said.

The Little Flower Girls' Hostel formed part of a huge mission station founded by Catholic missionaries at the turn of the century. Most of them were of European origin, but over the years the mission, set in the village of Asazi in Natal, had become a fully fledged community, producing its own breed of African nuns and priests from the surrounding villages.

Sister Marietta was a mouse-like creature of German origin. Armed with a bible and a strict Catholic upbringing, she was determined to save the whole African continent from death and destruction. Her biggest challenge while at The Little Flower was to keep the girls away from the evil clutches of men. Old Marie, as the girls referred to her, made it her business to slot in her anti-male propaganda whenever she could. Her best perform-

11

ances were a day or two before we broke up for the school holidays. She seemed to think that a good dose of lecturing would protect us from the menacing world outside.

She marvelled at the story of a boy who once cast a spell on a girl by simply looking at her. The girl, she said, had trusted her own worldly strength instead of asking for protection from the Virgin Mary. The boy had looked at the girl, the story went, and, without him saying a word, the girl had felt weak. So weak was she that, of her own accord, without the boy even propositioning her, she asked him to 'please kiss me and carry me to the bush'.

'I need not tell you what happened in the bush,' the nun would conclude.

As a rule, anyone who was caught eyeing the boys, whether in church, in class, or in the street, was punished severely. Ten bad marks in Sister Marietta's black book was the highest number one could get at a go, and they indicated the seriousness of the crime. As a result, trying to avoid boys and not being seen with them in a lonely place became our biggest challenge at The Little Flower.

'They will take you and use you, leaving you an empty shell,' Sister Marietta would say, indicating with her hand how a girl would be tossed away as something useless. So ominous was the prospect of being thrown away as a useless shell that Tosh and I would spend long nights discussing ways and means to avoid being subjected to that kind of treatment. Although we did not admire Sister Marietta personally, the idea of being sinless and celibate appealed to us a great deal. Often our night sessions would end with us saying the rosary together, asking for forgiveness for sins we had never committed.

Anastasia, Tasi to her friends, was the most popular girl at The Little Flower. While the rest of the girls loved and admired her, Tosh and I despised her. She dressed in the best fashion clothes, and had all the answers to life's problems. A dark person by nature, Tasi relied on skin-lightening cream to make her skin look lighter. So light was her face at one stage that her ebony hands looked borrowed next to it. Somehow her ears never got lighter, no matter how much cream she used on them. They stuck out like little appendages above her oval face. Tosh and I laughed about her ears behind her back. We did not dare do so

12

in her presence. Tasi's tongue was much too scathing.

'I wonder how Old Marie can be so knowledgeable about matters of the flesh when she has never been involved in them,' Tasi would say mockingly. 'She must be displacing her own fears and using us to fight her own inward physical desire. Celibacy . . . what nonsense. Old Marie must be jealous of our freedom. After all, *we* never sent her to tie herself to a life devoid of male pleasure.'

Tasi had quite a following, and her bed, which was at the corner of the hundred-bed dormitory, became the girls' rendez-vous. This was where all subjects ranging from politics to sex were discussed. Tasi owned a small transistor radio, and often her gang would convene at her bed to listen to the 'Hit Parade'. This had to happen behind Sister Marietta's back because to her, love and rock 'n roll constituted mortal sins. Often the music-listening session would end in a row, with the participants arguing about the lyrics of a song, or which song had been number one on the 'Hit Parade' the previous week.

It was at the rendezous that the anti-missionary politics were discussed. As far as Tasi was concerned, the missionaries, and that included Sister Marietta, had left Europe because of frustration, hunger and poverty. 'Under the guise of Christianity, they came to save us. Save us from what? When they themselves are guilty of racism and bigotry?' Tasi would ask, pointing at the stone building in which the black nuns were housed.

The Little Flower was not immune from the country's racial laws, which decreed that blacks and whites live separately. The white missionaries were clearly a privileged class. They lived in a glass building at the top of the hill, while their black counterparts were housed in a stone and brick building at the bottom of the hill. It looked more like a cave than a hut and, because of the density of the trees around it, it was cold and dark in winter.

Politics was a sacred subject at The Little Flower, and Tasi was the only one who openly challenged the racism of the convent. 'If they were like Jesus, they would be defying the laws of the country,' Tasi would say angrily. When Tasi questioned the school principal at assembly one day, we feared that she would be expelled from school. She was not. Instead she was fobbed off with an 'it was not the policy of the church to get

13

involved in politics' statement, and asked never to bring the subject up again. That did not deter Tasi. She continued to question and attack what she termed inexcusable behaviour from the people of God.

It was at the rendezvous that a perfect plan for smuggling letters was hatched. As a rule, letters sent in and out of the convent were read and censored by Sister Marietta. Incoming parcels were opened too, and every little gift considered to be too fancy for life in a convent school was kept, and not given to the owner until we broke up for the school holidays.

Love story books were banned from the library, and any pages with kissing couples, or people holding hands, were either cut out or blocked with paper. The same applied to movies. Scenes which were remotely sexual were edited out of the movie. We were allowed to watch *The Sound of Music* in my matric class. The movie was so butchered that when I saw it again a couple of years later, it looked completely new.

The smuggling of letters to and from the boys' side took place during morning mass. As the heads bowed down in silent prayer after holy communion, letters would be thrown across the aisle dividing the boys' from the girls' pews. The little pieces of paper, which for some reason were called schemes, would fly like missiles right above the nuns' heads.

One day a scheme which was thrown from the girls' to the boys' side landed right in the lap of Sister Marietta. Her face lit up with glee as she pocketed the letter, waiting for the perfect moment to pounce on the culprit. By the time she did, the school was buzzing with the news of the person who had been found with a scheme. Most of us were not sure who it was, but we were sympathetic because we knew what this would mean.

I had always suspected Sister Marietta to have a mean streak, but I never thought her capable of doing what she did with Thoko's letter. Of course Thoko's boyfriend denied any association between them, so she had to face the music alone.

Not only was the letter read to the whole school, it was sent home to her parents, with a letter instructing them to arrive at the school to reprimand Thoko 'or else she will be asked to pack her things and go'.

I could not understand how a private thing such as a letter could be read to the whole school. That convinced me that Sister

Marietta was downright malicious, doing that kind of thing to a nice girl like Thoko. Though remote, the thought of becoming a nun had often crossed my mind. What made me hesitate, however, was my mother's deep and sincere wish that I become a nurse. She would have been disappointed if I had gone the way of celibacy. Old Marie made the decision for me. Her reaction to Thoko's letter dashed my wish of ever becoming a nun. I was disgusted.

Tasi teased Thoko for having allowed herself to be caught with the letter. To her it was a big joke, and her friends laughed heartily when she described how foolish Thoko had been.

'There are only two rules,' Tasi said jokingly, 'it is either you keep away from trouble, or get involved, but be smart enough not to get caught.'

Tasi always boasted about how she and her boyfriend Michael smooched right under the nose of the Virgin Mary. She was referring to the statue of Mary on the lawn outside the school's courtyard. For those who had guts like Tasi, the grotto was a perfect lovers' nook.

More than once I heard Tasi tell the story of how she and Michael had climbed into one of the church towers. 'We stood there kissing to the chime of the bells next to us, while the priests heard confessions in the church below. Old Marie herself was playing the organ!' Tasi boasted. 'We did not get caught. What fool has any business to be caught?'

The stigma of being a boy's love followed Thoko until she left The Little Flower. She was banned from going to the movies on Fridays, and all the newcomers were warned that she was a bad influence. With the interesting parts censored out of all movies, Thoko didn't miss much, but it was the boring evenings that drove her nuts.

Thoko's every mistake became a big issue. She was ostracised by the rest of the girls who feared reprisals from Old Marie. As punishment for an offence Thoko was made to clean the local graveyard. It was not so much the hard work which caused grave-cleaning to be regarded as the most severe form of punishment. According to African culture graves are sacred ground where children are not allowed unless they are there to bury a very close relative such as a brother, a sister, or a parent. When Old Marie sent Thoko to dig round the graves for the second time, Tasi suggested we send a delegation to her to protest, and to make it clear what our tradition was regarding being in the cemetery.

'It is a bad omen, and shows no regard for our culture,' Tasi had protested. Although the delegation was given a hearing, their arguments were dismissed as primitive and unchristian, and Thoko was sent to clean up the graves a third and a fourth time. Such punishment was meted out to various other people, but Tasi vowed she would rather pack her bags and leave The Little Flower than dig round the graves. As if to avoid a confrontation, Old Marie never gave her the grave-digging punishment, robbing the girls of a chance to witness a showdown.

Once Sister Marietta embarrassed Thoko by pulling out the hem of her dress, saying that her dress was too short. As a rule, dresses had to be an inch above the knee. Thoko's must have been slightly more than an inch. The poor girl had to walk around with a funny dress the whole day because Sister would not let her change into another. It was her way of punishing her for, according to her mind, trying to be attractive to the opposite sex. But trying to make Thoko unattractive was an impossible task. Besides her God-given beauty, Thoko had natural style which made her look good with or without a torn hem. She looked elegant even in her gym slip, and Sister Marietta hated her for that. So intense was her hatred that she was forever looking for a reason for her to be expelled from school. 'You will dig the graves for a week, or pack your things and leave The Little Flower,' became the nun's familiar cry whenever Thoko did something wrong.

Tosh and I were both eighteen when we left The Little Flower. As we hugged and said goodbye, we renewed the vow we had made so many times before. If we ever slept with a boy, we would write or telephone to say we had finally fallen. I do not know exactly what motivated Tosh to make that vow. But for me, it was Thoko's experience that pushed me and forced me to make that decision. If a love letter could elicit so much hatred and anger, I thought to myself, then surely boys must be a real threat to girls. I sincerely believed that there would be no place for me in the world if I ever fell into the trap which every man around had set to catch me. As Old Marie said, 'The world will spit at you.'

16

Twenty years have passed since I last saw Tosh. I [...]
to find her after my first encounter with a man. I did no[...]
urge to write to her and tell her that I had finally fallen. [...]
mind, it had not happened. I remember the incident very clea[...]
It was on the couch in my mother's own lounge, not even in th[...]
bush as Sister Marietta had warned. Because he was Catholic
like me, I trusted Sipho more than I would have trusted an
ordinary boy. Somehow, I thought he knew the same rules that I
knew.

He pleaded with me and told me it would not take long. He
fondled my breasts and kissed me all over. I still cannot say
whether the feeling was pleasurable. It was as though a cold and
a warm shiver went through my body at the same time. I heard
two voices, that of Sipho in one ear pleading with me that 'it
won't be long', and Sister Marietta in another, warning 'it will
take two minutes'. I saw myself being discarded like an empty
shell and the whole world spitting at me.

Suddenly I fought like a little monster to push Sipho away. It
was too late. I heard him take one deep breath and the act was
over. It was exactly two minutes. I pulled myself together and
walked out of the door, leaving Sipho sitting on the couch. When
I walked away from him, I also walked away from the fact that
he had made love to me. As far as I was concerned the incident
had not happened. How could I admit that I had been used?

I have had a lot of sexual encounters since that day on my
mother's couch. I am married now with two children; still I have
not made love to a man. Sister Marietta never told me that there
would come a time when being in a lonely place with a boy
would be a right and a safe thing to do. So every private moment
I have spent with a man has been wrong, and something I have
to be ashamed of. Even as I go to bed with my husband every
night, Sister Marietta's voice rings in my mind. 'He will take you
and use you and throw you away like an empty shell.' When she
drummed those words into my innocent mind, she tied a knot
that I am now unable to undo.

How can I give myself on a platter to a person – a man – who
will con me and leave me spent and useless? As I pull myself
away from each sexual act, I feel used and unclean. A sense of
guilt and emptiness comes over me. Often I have felt the urge to
go back to The Little Flower, lock myself into a confessional

17

, 'Father, I have sinned. I have slept with

to Tosh to tell her that I have broken the
years ago. I have slept with none of the
to, none of the men I have met over the
be one day I will be able to untangle the
ind. I will be able to say to a man, 'Let us
sexual pot, let us share the pleasure
equally.' I will not write to Tosh. No, not until I reach equality
with my men. Tosh has not written either. Could it be that she is
plagued by the same anguish, or is she still pure?

did not try
feel the
o my

18

WHAT WERE YOU DREAMING?

Nadine Gordimer

I'm standing here by the road long time, yesterday, day before, today. Not the same road but it's the same – hot, hot like today. When they turn off to where they're going, I must get out again, wait again. Some of them they just pretend there's nobody there, they don't want to see nobody. Even go a bit faster, *ja*. Then they past, and I'm waiting. I combed my hair; I don't want to look like a *skolly*. Don't smile because they think you being too friendly, you think you good as them. They go and they go. Some's got the baby's napkin hanging over the back window to keep out this sun. Some's not going on holiday with their kids but is alone; all alone in a big car. But they'll never stop, the whites, if they alone. Never. Because these *skollies* and that kind've spoilt it all for us, sticking a gun in the driver's neck, stealing his money, beating him up and taking the car. Even killing him. So it's buggered up for us. No white wants some guy sitting behind his head. And the blacks – when they stop for you, they ask for money. They want you must pay, like for a taxi! The blacks!

But then these whites: they're stopping; I'm surprised, because it's only two – empty in the back – and the car it's a beautiful one. The windows are that special glass, you can't see in if you outside, but the woman has hers down and she's calling me over with her finger. She ask me where I'm going and I say the next place because they don't like to have you for too far, so she say get in and lean into the back to move along her stuff that's on the back seat to make room. Then she say, lock the door, just push that button down, we don't want you to fall out, and it's like she's joking with someone she know. The man driving smiles over his shoulder and say something – I can't hear it very well, it's the way he talk English. So anyway I say what's all right to

19

say, yes master, thank you master, I'm going to Warmbad. He ask again, but man, I don't get it – *Ekskuus*? Please? And she chips in – she's a lady with grey hair and he's a young chap – My friend's from England, he's asking if you've been waiting a long time for a lift. So I tell them – A long time? Madam! And because they white, I tell them about the blacks, how when they stop they ask you to pay. This time I understand what the young man's saying, he say, And most whites don't stop? And I'm careful what I say, I tell them about the blacks, how too many people spoilt it for us, they robbing and killing, you can't blame white people. Then he ask where I'm from. And she laugh and look round where I'm behind her. I see she know I'm from the Cape, although she ask me. I tell her I'm from the Cape Flats and she say she suppose I'm not born there, though, and she's right, I'm born in Wynberg, right there in Cape Town. So she say, And they moved you out?

Then I catch on what kind of white she is; so I tell her, yes, the government kicked us out from our place, and she say to the young man, You see?

He want to know why I'm not in the place in the Cape Flats, why I'm so far away here. I tell them I'm working in Pietersburg. And he keep on, why? Why? What's my job, everything, and if I don't understand the way he speak, she chips in again all the time and ask me for him. So I tell him, panel beater. And I tell him, the pay is very low in the Cape. And then I begin to tell them lots of things, some things is real and some things I just think of, things that are going to make them like me, maybe they'll take me all the way there to Pietersburg.

I tell them I'm six days on the road. I not going to say I'm sick as well, I been home because I was sick – because *she's* not from overseas, I suss that, she know that old story. I tell them I had to take leave because my mother's got trouble with my brothers and sisters, we seven in the family and no father. And s'true's God, it seem like what I'm saying. When do you ever see him except he's drunk. And my brother is trouble, trouble, he hangs around with bad people and my other brother doesn't help my mother. And that's no lie, neither, how can he help when he's doing time; but they don't need to know that, they only get scared I'm the same kind like him, if I tell about him, assault and intent to do bodily harm. The sisters are in school and my mother's only got the pension. *Ja.* I'm working there in Pietersburg and every week, madam, I swear to you, I send my pay for my mother and sisters. So then he say, Why get off here? Don't you want us to take you to Pietersburg? And she say, of course, they going that way.

And I tell them some more. They listening to me so nice, and I'm talking, talking. I talk about the government, because I hear she keep saying to him, telling about this law and that law. I say how it's not fair we had to leave Wynberg and go to the Flats. I tell her we got sicknesses – she say what kind, is it unhealthy here? And I don't have to think what, I just say it's *bad, bad*, and she say to the man, *As I told you.* I tell about the house we had in Wynberg, but it's not my grannie's old house where we was all living together so long, the house I'm telling them about is more the kind of house they'll know, they wouldn't like to go away from, with a tiled bathroom, electric stove, everything, I tell them we spend three thousand rands fixing up that house – my uncle give us the money, that's how we got it. He give us his savings, three thousand rands. (I don't know why I say three; old Uncle Jimmy never have three or two or one in his life. I just say it.) And then we just kicked out. And panel beaters getting low pay there; it's better in Pietersburg.

He say, but I'm far from my home? And I tell her again, because she's white but she's a woman too, with that grey hair she's got grown-up kids – Madam, I send my pay home every week, s'true's God, so's they can eat, there in the Flats. I'm saying, *six days on the road.* While I'm saying it, I'm thinking; then I say, look at me, I got only these clothes, I sold my things on the way, to have something to eat. *Six days on the road.* He's from overseas and she isn't one of those who say you're a liar, doesn't trust you – right away when I got in the car, I notice she doesn't take her stuff over to the front like they usually do in case you pinch something of theirs. Six days on the road, and am I tired, tired! When I get to Pietersburg I must try borrow me a rand to get a taxi there to where I live. He say, Where do you live? Not in town? And she laugh, because he don't know nothing about this place, where whites live and where we must go – but I know they both thinking and I know what they thinking; I know I'm going to get something when I get out, don't need to worry about that. They feel bad about me, now.

21

Bad. Anyhow it's God's truth that I'm tired, tired, that's true.

They've put up her window and he's pushed a few buttons, now it's like in a supermarket, cool air blowing, and the windows like sunglasses: that sun can't get me here.

The Englishman glances over his shoulder as he drives.

'Taking a nap.'

'I'm sure it's needed.'

All through the trip he stops for everyone he sees at the roadside. Some are not hitching at all, never expecting to be given a lift anywhere, just walking in the heat outside with an empty plastic can to be filled with water or paraffin or whatever it is they buy in some country store, or standing at some point between departure and destination, small children and bundles linked on either side, baby on back. She hasn't said anything to him. He would only misunderstand if she explained why one doesn't give lifts in this country; and if she pointed out that in spite of this, she doesn't mind him breaking the sensible if unfortunate rule, he might misunderstand that, as well – think she was boasting of her disregard for personal safety weighed in the balance against decent concern for fellow beings.

He persists in making polite conversation with these passengers because he doesn't want to be patronizing; picking them up like so many objects and dropping them off again, silent, smelling of smoke from open cooking fires, sun and sweat, there behind his head. They don't understand his Englishman's English and if he gets an answer at all it's a deaf man's guess at what's called for. Some grin with pleasure, and embarrass him by showing it the way they've been taught is acceptable, invoking him as *baas* and *master* when they get out and give thanks. But although he doesn't know it, being too much concerned with those names thrust into his hands like whips whose purpose is repugnant to him, has nothing to do with him, she knows each time that there is a moment of annealment in the air-conditioned hired car belonging to nobody – a moment like that on a no-man's-land bridge in which an accord between warring countries is signed – when there is no calling of names, and all belong in each other's presence. He doesn't feel it because he has no wounds, nor has inflicted, nor will inflict any.

This one standing at the roadside with his transistor radio in a plastic bag was actually thumbing a lift like a townee; his expectation marked him out. And when her companion to whom she was showing the country inevitably pulled up, she read the face at the roadside immediately: the lively, cajoling, performer's eyes, the salmon-pinkish cheeks and nostrils, and as he jogged over smiling, the unselfconscious gap of gum between the canines.

A sleeper is always absent; although present, there on the back seat.

'The way he spoke about black people, wasn't it surprising? I mean – he's black himself.'

'Oh no he's not. Couldn't you see the difference? He's a Cape Coloured. From the way he speaks English – couldn't you hear he's not like the Africans you've talked to?'

But of course he hasn't seen, hasn't heard: the fellow is dark enough, to those who don't know the signs by which you're classified, and the melodramatic, long-vowelled English is as difficult to follow if more fluent than the terse, halting responses of blacker people.

'Would he have a white grandmother or even a white father, then?'

She gives him another of the little history lessons she has been supplying along the way. The Malay slaves brought by the Dutch East India Company to their supply station, on the route to India, at the Cape in the seventeenth century; the Hottentots who were the indigenous inhabitants of that part of Africa; add Dutch, French, English, German settlers whose backyard progeniture with these and other blacks began a people who are all the people in the country mingled in one bloodstream. But encounters along the road teach him more than her history lessons, or the political analyses in which they share the same ideological approach although he does not share responsibility for the experience to which the ideology is being applied. She has explained Acts, Proclamations, Amendments. The Group Areas Act, Resettlement Act, Orderly Movement and Settlement of Black Persons Act. She has translated these statute book euphemisms: people as movable goods. People packed onto trucks along with their stoves and beds while front-end loaders scoop away their homes into rubble. People dumped somewhere else. Always somewhere else. People as the figures, decimal

23

points and multiplying zero-zero-zeros into which individual lives – Black Persons Orderly-Moved, -Effluxed, -Grouped – coagulate and compute. Now he has here in the car the intimate weary odour of a young man to whom these things happen.

'Half his family sick . . . it must be pretty unhealthy, where they've been made to go.'

She smiles. 'Well, I'm not too sure about that. I had the feeling, some of what he said . . . they're theatrical by nature. You must take it with a pinch of salt.'

'You mean about the mother and sisters and so on?'

She's still smiling, she doesn't answer.

'But he couldn't have made up about taking a job so far from home – and the business of sending his wages to his mother? That too?'

He glances at her.

Beside him, she's withdrawn as the other one, sleeping behind him. While he turns his attention back to the road, she is looking at him secretly, as if somewhere in his blue eye registering the approaching road but fixed on the black faces he is trying to read, somewhere in the lie of his inflamed hand and arm that on their travels have been plunged in the sun as if in boiling water, there is the place through which the worm he needs to be infected with can find a way into him, so that he may host it and become its survivor, himself surviving through being fed on. Become like her. Complicity is the only understanding.

'Oh it's true, it's all true . . . not in the way he's told about it. Truer than the way he told it. All these things happen to them. And other things. Worse. But why burden us? Why try to explain to us? Things so far from what we know, how will they ever explain? How will we react? Stop our ears? Or cover our faces? Open the door and throw him out? They don't know. But sick mothers and brothers gone to the bad – these are the staples of misery, mmh? Think of the function of charity in the class struggles in your own country in the nineteenth century; it's all there in your literature. The lord-of-the-manor's compassionate daughter carrying hot soup to the dying cottager on her father's estate. The 'advanced' upper-class woman comforting her cook when the honest drudge's daughter takes to whoring for a living. *Shame*, we say here. Shame. You must've heard it? We think it means, what a pity; we think we are expressing sympathy – for

24

them. *Shame*. I don't know what we're saying about ourselves.'
She laughs.

'So you think it would at least be true that his family were
kicked out of their home, sent away?'

'Why would anyone of them need to make that up? It's an
everyday affair.'

'What kind of place would they get, where they were moved?'

'Depends. A tent, to begin with. And maybe basic materials to
build themselves a shack. Perhaps a one-room prefab. Always a
tin toilet set down in the veld, if nothing else. Some industrialist
must be making a fortune out of government contracts for those
toilets. You build your new life round the toilet. His people are
Coloured, so it could be they were sent where there were houses
of some sort already built for them; Coloureds usually get
something a bit better than blacks are given.'

'And the house would be more or less as good as the one they
had? People as poor as that – and they'd spent what must seem a
fortune to them, fixing it up.'

'I don't know what kind of house they had. We're not talking
about slum clearance, my dear; we're talking about destroying
communities because they're black, and white people want to
build houses or factories for whites where blacks live. I told you.
We're talking about loading up trucks and carting black people
out of sight of whites.'

'And even where he's come to work – Pietersburg, whatever-
it's-called – he doesn't live in the town.'

'Out of sight.' She has lost the thought for a moment,
watching to make sure the car takes the correct turning. 'Out of
sight. Like those mothers and grannies and brothers and sisters
far away on the Cape Flats.'

'I don't think it's possible he actually sends all his pay. I mean
how would one eat?'

'Maybe what's left doesn't buy anything he really wants.'

Not a sound, not a sigh in sleep, behind them. They can go on
talking about him as he always has been discussed, there and yet
not there.

Her companion is alert to the risk of gullibility. He verifies the
facts, smiling, just as he converts, mentally, into pounds and pence
any sum spent in foreign coinage. 'He didn't sell the radio. When he
said he'd sold all his things on the road, he forgot about that.'

25

'When did he say he'd last eaten?'

'Yesterday. He said.'

She repeats what she has just been told: 'Yesterday.' She is looking through the glass that takes the shine of heat off the landscape passing as yesterday passed, time measured by the ticking second-hand of moving trees, rows of crops, country-store stoeps, filling stations, spiny crook'd fingers of giant euphorbia. Only the figures by the roadside waiting, standing still.

Personal remarks can't offend someone dead-beat in the back. 'How d'you think such a young man comes to be without front teeth?'

She giggles whisperingly and keeps her voice low, anyway. 'Well, you may not believe me if I tell you . . .'

'Seems odd . . . I suppose he can't afford to have them replaced.'

'It's – how shall I say – a sexual preference. Most usually you see it in their young girls, though. They have their front teeth pulled when they're about seventeen.'

She feels his uncertainty, his not wanting to let comprehension lead him to a conclusion embarrassing to an older woman. For her part, she is wondering whether he won't find it distasteful if – at her de-sexed age – she should come out with it: for cock-sucking. 'No-one thinks the gap spoils a girl's looks, apparently. It's simply a sign she knows how to please. Same significance between men, I suppose. . . . A form of beauty. So everyone says. We've always been given to understand that's the reason.'

'Maybe it's just another sexual myth. There are so many.'

She's in agreement. 'Black girls. Chinese girls. Jewish girls.'

'And black men?'

'Oh my goodness, you bet. But we white ladies don't talk about that, we only dream, you know! Or have nightmares.'

They're laughing. When they are quiet, she flexes her shoulders against the seat-back and settles again. The streets of a town are flickering their text across her eyes. 'He might have had a car accident. They might have been knocked out in a fight.'

They have to wake him because they don't know where he wants to be set down. He is staring at her lined white face (turned to him, calling him gently), stunned for a moment at this evidence that he cannot be anywhere he ought to be; and now he blinks and smiles his empty smile caught on either side by a canine tooth, and gulps and gives himself a shake like someone coming out of water. 'Sorry! Sorry! Sorry madam!'

What about, she says, and the young man glances quickly, his blue eyes coming round over his shoulder: 'Had a good snooze?'

'Ooh I was finished, master, finished, God bless you for the rest you give me. And with an empty stummick, you know, you dreaming so real. I was dreaming, dreaming, I didn't know nothing about I'm in the car!'

It comes from the driver's seat with the voice (a real Englishman's, from overseas) of one who is hoping to hear something that will explain everything. 'What were you dreaming?'

But there is only hissing, spluttery laughter between the two white pointed teeth. The words gambol. 'Ag, nothing, master, nothing, all *non*-sunce – '

The sense is that if pressed, he will produce for them a dream he didn't dream, a dream put together from bloated images on billboards, discarded calendars picked up, scraps of newspapers blown about – but they interrupt, they're asking where he'd like to get off.

'No, anywhere. Here it's all right. Fine. Just there by the corner. I must go look for someone who'll praps give me a rand for the taxi, because I can't walk so far, I haven't eaten nothing since yesterday . . . just here, the master can please stop just here – '

The traffic light is red, anyway, and the car is in the lane nearest the kerb. Her thin, speckled white arm with a skilled flexible hand but no muscle with which to carry a load of washing or lift a hoe, feels back to release the lock he is fumbling at. 'Up, up, pull it up.' She has done it for him. 'Can't you take a bus?'

'There's no buses Sunday, madam, this place is ve-ery bad for us for transport, I must tell you, we can't get nowhere Sundays, only work-days.' He is out, the plastic bag with the radio under his arm, his feet in their stained, multi-striped jogging sneakers drawn neatly together like those of a child awaiting dismissal. 'Thank you, madam, thank you master. God bless you for what you done.'

The confident dextrous hand is moving quickly down in the

straw bag bought from a local market somewhere along the route. She brings up a pale blue note (the Englishman recognizes the two-rand denomination of this currency that he has memorized by colour) and turns to pass it, a surreptitious message, through the open door behind her. *Goodbye master madam*. The note disappears delicately as a titbit finger-fed. He closes the door, he's keeping up the patter, *goodbye master, goodbye madam*, and she instructs – 'No, bang it. Harder. That's it.' *Goodbye master, goodbye madam* – but they don't look back at him now, they don't have to see him thinking he must keep waving, keep smiling, in case they should look back.

She is the guide and mentor; she's the one who knows the country. She's the one – she knows that too – who is accountable. She must be the first to speak again. 'At least if he's hungry he'll be able to buy a bun or something. And the bars are closed on Sunday.'

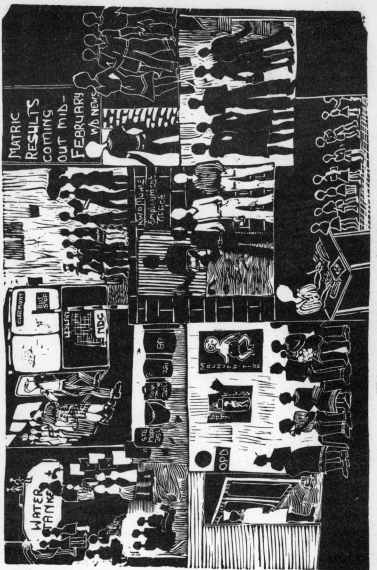

Waiting . . . waiting . . . people waiting

ONE LAST LOOK AT PARADISE ROAD

Gladys Thomas

Miriam, not knowing where to start, looked wearily around the house at her duties for the day. Washing lay on the bedroom floor ready for the automatic washing machine. Dishes were piled high in the kitchen sink indicating that a good time was had by all at Madam's party. After she had served dinner to the guests last night, she had left the kitchen about nine o'clock. Most nights she would spend with her friend who worked across the road. They would talk about their families, their Madams and everything that affected their lives. Last night, however, Miriam had felt too tired and just fell asleep in her tiny room. This morning she was back in the big house to do the cleaning up!

Today her heart felt heavy in her breast. She was nervous and had dropped things. Already she had broken a porcelain figurine when she was dusting. Tonight she would have to face the consequences. All she could do, as was usual after such a confrontation, was to return to the lonely maid's room in the back yard, and sulk.

She carried a transistor radio from room to room while doing her chores. She was listening expectantly for news of the worsening unrest in the townships. And it was a special day because of the call to march to Pollsmoor Prison to demand the release of Nelson Mandela. Why could she not be with her family and her people at a time like this? Instead she was compelled to spend her time cleaning for the rich and unconcerned.

At eleven-thirty she heard those special bleeps on the radio which preceeded the news. Anxiously she turned up the sound for the urgent news flash. The police had taken over Athlone and the march on Pollsmoor had been put to an abrupt end! The police had used batons, quirts and teargas. There were many injured and detained.

Mirian stood stunned and shocked because some of the reported incidents had taken place near her home. After a while she decided that it would be best to return to the township where she lived, to where she felt that she would be needed by her family and neighbours. She filled the dog's water bowl, kicked the washing into a corner, locked all the doors, and left the big house in a hurry.

As she locked the gate she remembered that Madam would certainly telephone that afternoon to enquire, as she usually did, about what she would be cooking for supper that night. Now that was the least of her worries – she was on her way home!

She walked as quickly as her ungainly tired body could carry her. She turned into Paradise Road which was lined with tall green oak trees; birds flew about, and squirrels with their frenetic bushy tails jumped along the branches. The avenue, so peaceful with its beautiful spring-green trees stretching almost as far as the eye could see, was just like some fabled Eden.

Almost breathless, she arrived at the Claremont bus terminus and was just in time for a departing bus to her township. She had little time to waste as she had to return to her work before the white family arrived home that night. She sat down resolutely in a vacant seat at the window. As she stared out she thought about her husband, Amos. Yes, together they had been through hard times bringing up their three children; both working to make ends meet until three months ago when he was brought home in one of the construction company's trucks. The driver had to carry him inside the house! He had been employed by the company for ten years. Yet the day he injured himself the foreman said that he was too busy to fill in the compensation forms! Until now he had received just two weeks' pay and a pair of crutches.

These thoughts made her angry and, given the opportunity, she would have walked in the front row of that march! But she could not stay at home as she needed the job so badly. The family depended on the hundred-and-twenty rand a month which she earned as a maid. She thought about her daughter Winnie, the other breadwinner of the family. She worked at Groote Schuur Hospital as a trainee nurse. Every month Winnie

31

would bring home her pay packet unopened. Miriam was very proud of her and loved her very much.

Her two sons were now both at high school. Ah, how she adored them! They never complained and were always satisfied. They wore patched pants and their shoes were often down at heel, but they never missed school. She really admired them and their dedication to their studies.

Steve was now in his final matriculation year and her baby, Fassie, now sixteen, was in Standard Eight. They were both so bright that she smiled as she thought about them. They would have joined the march that morning as they were supporters of the People's United Front. She remembered how her boys insisted on taking her to the mass political rally at the skating rink in Athlone. She had never seen such a crowd in her life! All were meeting for the struggle for freedom. The speeches were fiery and pertinent about the oppressive laws of her cruel country. She had felt pleased that her sons had brought her to the rally.

She was so deep in thought that she almost missed her stop. As she alighted, stones came smashing into the bus windows. The driver in great fear jumped out and ran for his life. Everyone scattered as the stones rained down upon the bus. Some of the youths were shouting slogans and angry words; 'Down with the bus fares!', 'We did not ask to be here!', 'The government moved us to this ghetto!' They shouted at the empty bus as if it had ears! Missiles were aimed at the bright smiling face of a girl advertising toothpaste on the side of the bus. The stones smashed into the face with dull thuds. She saw flames quickly consume the smiling face leaving the side of the bus a blackened charred mass. Soon the whole bus was burning fiercely, as she hurried home, shocked at what she had witnessed.

The township looked like a battlefield. Clumsy-looking troop-carriers called Casspirs, army trucks filled with troops armed to the teeth and police with guns were to be seen everywhere. A soldier in full battledress and riot gear came towards her. Her heart began to pound fast and in a panic she half ran home. Children and adults were being chased like cornered animals. She turned a street corner; the teargas and burning tyres' smoke choked her as she stumbled into her home.

'Amos, Amos!' she cried and ran into the small dark bedroom. He stood at the window leaning on his crutches. They fell into each other's arms.

'I'm glad you're home, Mother. This all started this morning. It was going to be a peaceful march to Pollsmoor. Then came the batons and the guns. Standing here, and I'm unable to go out and help the injured, is driving me mad.'

'Where are the children?' she asked anxiously.

'They joined the march this morning. I never saw them after that.'

'Oh God, please bring them home safe. It is terrible out there and all we can do is just sit here while our children are fighting the whole army and all those guns. I feel so helpless, Amos.'

'I feel exactly the same, Miriam. I wish I had died in that accident!'

'Oh Amos, my husband. Why do you talk like that? Soon you will be strong and on your feet again. We must not give in now. Our children need our support. Come, let's see what there is to eat. What you need is a nice cup of tea.'

'Don't worry, my wife. You go and look for the boys. I can get something to eat for myself. Besides, I feel like being alone.'

'Why do you want to be alone? I've just come in from work to be with you, and you want to be alone?'

'I know your heart is out there with the boys. You go and look for them. I'll be all right.'

'Are you sure, Amos?' she asked tenderly.

She went to the kitchen to drink some water as her throat was irritated by the gas. She noticed that the boys had left in a great hurry – plates of half-eaten mealie meal still stood on the table. The large enamelled basin was filled with dirty dishes and the bucket that Fassie used to scrub the floor stood under the old wooden kitchen table. They had never before left for school before cleaning the house, but that morning was obviously an exception. She went back into the bedroom to tell Amos that she was leaving. As she turned away Amos looked sadly at her, thinking, 'We live in such dangerous times that you don't know if you'll see your loved ones again once they leave the house. Bloody murderers!'

Miriam reached the gate and then turned quickly back into the house. She stood in the doorway and shouted, 'Are you sure you're all right? Don't leave the house until I return. Do you hear me, Amos?'

'Go Wife, go! But take care. These people are out to kill us today.'

She rushed out into the street. Stones rained from behind walls and bushes. She had to dodge and run to avoid the missiles. There were tyres burning in the streets, barricading the way of the Casspirs. But the iron monsters moved forward relentlessly. The faces of the men on the Casspirs, she noticed, were red with anger. Thick palls of tearsmoke filled the air and the tyres gave off acrid fumes which inflamed the eyes and throat. She heard gunshots in the next street and the piercing cries of the children. It was like a nightmare as she made her way to her sister's home a few streets away. She found herself running with the crowd at times. Perhaps her sons were at their Aunt Susan's home, hiding?

As she entered Susan's home she immediately felt that something was amiss. She found her in the kitchen shaking in a panic. Holding her ten-month-old baby over the kitchen sink she was blowing air into the child's mouth. This beautiful child with her large brown eyes, who was always gurgling with delight, now lay limp in her mother's arms!

'What happened?' Miriam asked very alarmed.

'They threw a teargas canister through the doorway. Little Dolly had just crawled there to sit in the sun,' answered Susan, tears running down her cheeks. 'My baby almost choked to death.'

'Give her to me,' said Miriam, and she held the child to her body. Slowly she rocked Dolly while her sister wiped the little face with a wet cold face cloth.

'I'm looking for Steve and Fassie. They didn't attend school today but joined the march. I thought they may be here with you, Sister.'

'I didn't see them today, Miriam. Where can they be? Perhaps they're hiding someplace.'

'But I want to find them before I go back to my work this evening.'

'Are you off today?'

'I decided to come home when I heard the news of the beatings on the radio.'

34

'Why didn't they allow this peaceful march?' Susan asked angrily.

'Yes, they want to shoot all of us,' anwered Miriam. 'Here, I think she's sleeping,' Miriam handed Dolly back to Susan. 'You must watch her, anything can happen. I must leave now and search for the boys. Keep your door closed,' she warned as she left.

Back on the streets she followed the crowd. By now her heavy body felt tired and sweaty. She ran along searching the crowd for her sons' faces amongst them. They were all singing freedom songs but nowhere did she see Steve or Fassie. The faces of the youth shocked her. She detected signs of hope, determination and defiance in them. On the way she met many mothers and stopped to talk to some of them that she knew.

'I'm looking for my sons,' she tried to explain. They ignored her in their rush to get away.

'No time to talk,' said one of the young men in the crowd.

'Come on, Mama. If you stand too long in one place they will shoot you,' said another.

She joined the others, half running and half walking. Passing another woman she asked, 'Are you also looking for your children?'

'Yes, yes!' several of the mothers in the crowd answered in great apprehension.

'Not one of them are at school today.'

'They say that they are doing what we should have done years ago.'

'That's true,' approved several women.

When she approached her street she said goodbye to them and returned home very disappointed.

'Miriam, Miriam. Is it you?' Amos called from the bedroom. 'Did you find them?'

'Oh, Amos. You'll never believe what's going on out there! It seems that all the high school students joined the march this morning. I tell you Amos, these children don't care about their lives!' She was now so overcome that she just sat down on the bed, crying.

'All right, Mother. Don't worry! It will turn out all right. I know it,' he pacified her.

'I will not go back to work until I've found my sons,' she said between her tears.

'What if you lose your job?'

'We will manage on Winnie's money. We've been through worse times before. But I'm going to stay here where I belong. Let the rich do their own work for a change. I'm tired of cooking, cleaning and picking up after them. I hate them all! They couldn't care a damn about us.'

'My wife, you've been running around since this morning,' said Amos looking at her with great concern. 'Come let me make that cup of tea we were going to have this morning.' He shuffled into the kitchen followed by Miriam.

'You must rest that leg of yours. Let me make the tea instead and I'll tell you what is going on out there. The children are all over the township. The roads are blocked with old mattresses and oil drums. I saw some of them making petrol bombs behind a wall. I can't believe it! There is a war going on out there, Amos.'

'And no sign of our sons? I'm sure they will come home soon.'

'Want some more tea?' she asked him. They continued to discuss the situation until late the afternoon.

Suddenly the front door burst open and about six young people stormed inside breathlessly, seeking a place to hide. With them was Steve. When he saw his mother he was visibly surprised.

'Mama, why are you home from your work?'

'How can I stay at work with all this happening here?'

All Steve's friends seemed extremely nervous and fearful and cast anxious looks towards the front door.

'We must hide in here. Away from the police, Ma! They're after us and they are going to kill us, Ma!'

'Kill? Not while I'm around.'

Amos suggested that two should hide behind the toilet in the back yard. They ran outside as fast as they could. Miriam pushed two boys into the bedroom. Steve and the last one jumped into the old fireplace which was covered by an old floral curtain. When they were safely in their hiding places, Miriam poked her head behind the curtain. 'Where is your brother, Fassie?'

'I don't know. Shuh! Please go away, Mama. We'll go and look for him later. Please go, Ma.' She returned to Amos and they stared at each other as a deathly silence fell over the house.

A loud crash preceded the front door being kicked open and in marched several policemen. They went straight into the kitchen without any invitation. Miriam's heart beat so fast that she could feel the colour warming her face, her hair soaked in sweat. Amos pretended that he was reading a book. It looked as if a blue-grey cloud of uniforms and hateful brown, black and red faces had invaded Miriam's kitchen. They confronted her and Amos with their guns at the ready. Miriam said a silent prayer.

'Where are they?' demanded the leader. 'We saw them come in this house,' he shouted at the two old people. His men backed him in unison.

'You saw wrong,' Miriam shouted back in the same tone, surprising even Amos with her courage. 'There is no one in this house but myself and my husband. How do you know they came here? All these council houses look the same.'

'Search the whole place! And outside in the yard,' the big red bull bellowed to his men.

They kicked over the dustbin in the yard. They threw everything around with absolute contempt. The men inside were deliberately knocking over chairs and one officer ripped the curtains from the windows, declaring, 'This bloody house is as dark as hell!' Others went kicking open the inside doors of the house, searching everywhere. One even turned over the old zinc bath which the family used for their weekly bath. He flung it to the cement floor so that it made the sound of a bomb going off in the room. They appeared to be pleased with the chaos they were causing. But they did not discover any of the children! One of the policemen returned: 'There is only that old stink shithouse out there.'

'Where are they?' the sergeant shouted at Amos in anger and pulled at his crutch. Amos almost fell and a sharp pain shot up his bad leg. Miriam quickly held on to him.

'We don't know. We are alone here, my Baas,' he whimpered.

On hearing the word 'Baas' the sergeant looked pleased, thinking that he was in control of the situation. He called his men and ordered them to stop the search. The house was a shambles when they marched out. 'We will be back,' shouted the sergeant over his shoulder.

As a parting gift one of the policemen threw a teargas canister into the kitchen. Miriam and Amos struggled towards the

37

bedroom to save themselves from choking. After shutting the bedroom door behind them they fell down on to the bed, bewildered. Every room in the house was soon filled with tearsmoke. Miriam had grabbed a wet facecloth from behind the bedroom door and held it over Amos's face as he had seemed to faint. Quickly she opened the bedroom window. 'They are pigs. Just smell this house! Are you all right?' she asked Amos.

'We must live like this because we are of the wrong colour, Mother.'

One by one the boys crept out of their hiding places and thanked Miriam and Amos politely, almost apologetically, for the trouble they had caused. Miriam ordered them to open all the windows and doors to get the smell out of the house. 'It's our duty to protect you children,' said Miriam.

The children discussed the events of the day in the backroom where Steve and Fassie slept. In their bedroom Miriam and Amos sat in silence. Finally she asked, 'Where is our Fassie?'

'I hope he is safe,' answered Amos. She started to weep softly. After a while she knelt down to pray at his side. Amos tenderly laid his hand on her while the young people continued their meeting. Their loud and angry voices filtered through to the bedroom.

'I saw them baton charge a young girl as she lay on the ground.'

'That policeman hit her over the body with the strength of an ox!' said Steve.

'I saw them whip a priest full in the face, shattering his spectacles. I'm sure he's lost the sight in that eye. I've never seen anything so cruel,' said another.

'What about the two old nuns they arrested!' someone complained angrily.

'All our leaders have been detained. Tomorrow we will meet at school and decide how to protest against this injustice,' said Steve.

'One of you go outside and see if the police vans are still patrolling. We must search for my brother. We must find him!'

As they prepared to leave, their lookout returned to whisper, 'It's all clear. They've left the area.'

On the way out Steve went into his parents' room. His father was asleep but his mother was sitting next to him, just staring into space. 'We are going to look for Fassie, Ma. You rest now, I can see that you are tired.'

'God go with you, Son.' She lay down next to her husband, but she was awake for a long time still. In the distance she heard the sound of gunshots, and people running and screaming.

The following morning she awoke with a headache and her body felt stiff all over. Quietly she tiptoed into the next room to see if Steve had returned home the previous night. On seeing the sleeping figure she murmured, 'Thank God.' Miriam shook him awake, asking softly, 'Do you have any news about your brother?'

'We've looked all over, Ma. But he cannot be found.'

Miriam went silently into the kitchen to cook a pot of mealie meal for breakfast. As she stirred the porridge she decided to go to Groote Schuur Hospital to tell Winnie about Fassie's disappearance.

'Maybe she can help,' she said to herself. After they had had their breakfast Steve prepared to leave for school.

'I'm going to Winnie for help. Maybe Fassie is in hospital,' Miriam stated.

'Take care how you walk, Ma. Don't take chances out there,' said Steve. 'I'm off now. 'Bye Ma and Pa. Take care now,' he shouted on his way out.

'I must be off too,' Miriam said to Amos.

'Will you be all right or shall I come with you?'

'Now how can you come with your injured leg? No, you stay here. I won't be long.' She pulled a scarf over her head, kissed him and left the house with feelings of anticipation that she would somehow find Fassie.

The streets were scattered with stones and the burnt-out tyres had left imprinted circles on the asphalt roads from the previous day's unrest. As she passed the high school she saw massive army trucks parked outside the grounds with police and soldiers patrolling inside the fence. Their rifles were hanging down their sides. A helicopter hovered overhead. A Buffel troop carrier appeared from around a corner like an angry buffalo with a cannon for a nose, ready to attack. The township looked like a battlefield and a deathly atmosphere pervaded the scene which seemed to expect more violence. She hurried on and when she arrived at the hospital she climbed the stairs to Ward T2 where Winnie was on duty. They embraced each other.

'You look terrible, Ma. Are Steve and Fassie okay?' Winnie asked anxiously.

'That's why I'm here. They joined the march to Pollsmoor yesterday. Now Fassie is missing. We are sick with worry.'

'Wait let me ask Matron for a few minutes off, then we can talk inside.'

After a short while Winnie returned and took her mother's arm. They went through the male wards of the hospital. Winnie searched among the faces of the patients for her brother's, but without success.

'Come let's go to the out-patients, Ma,' suggested Winnie. They found the corridors crowded with injured people from the townships. Inside the hall the benches were packed, and the doctors were busy attending to some people with gunshot wounds. A young boy howled for his mother. Winnie and Miriam walked amongst the injured people searching for Fassie but he was not to be found there.

Winnie saw her mother out, kissed her and promised to change her shift and come home as soon as possible. Miriam walked to the bus stop as if in a trance. After she had paid her fare, she counted the money in her purse. As there wasn't enough left for her to go straight home, she decided to collect her wages at the big house. However, to her surprise Steve was waiting for her at the Claremont bus terminus. Her heart started racing as he came towards her.

'What is it, Son?' she asked apprehensively.

'Fassie is on the run, Ma, ' he blurted out.

'Why, what happened?' she asked. 'What does it mean?'

'He threw a petrol bomb at a police van. They saw his face and gave chase. He hid in someone's house and then jumped the fences. They followed him. If they find him he will go to jail. They know who he is! We will just have to wait for him to return home when the time is right.'

'I thank the Lord, he is alive. When will this unrest end?' she cried.

'No one knows. Looks like it's only started.' Steve looked grim-faced.

'Look Steve, I have no more money. We need food. I'm going

to Madam to explain the situation to her. She will understand and give me my money. I'll go back to work when Fassie comes home. Now I must go to the big house. Are you coming with me, Steve?'

'No, Ma. I don't like it amongst those people. You go. I'll go home to Pa. But please bring some food home, Ma.'

They each went their own way, she back to Paradise Road and Steve back to the township.

As she opened the gate of her employer's home, the dog ran to meet her. She went around to the back door and in the yard, to her surprise, she met a new maid with a bucket and rags hanging from her arm.

'Is the Madam home?'

'Yes. She is drinking her tea on the patio,' the girl answered shyly.

Miriam walked through the huge house to the poolside. There she saw Madam sunbathing. She went closer, 'Good afternoon, Madam,' she said in a shaking voice. She didn't know how to go on.

Madam looked up and replied casually, 'Oh, you finally arrived, Miriam.'

In a defiant mood Miriam replied, 'I've had a lot of trouble, Madam. My son is gone. My Fassie is missing!'

'I believe there is unrest in all the townships. Why are you people so violent? And where is your son? He is supposed to be at school, not so?'

'I see someone has already taken my place. Why the hurry?'

'Well, you let me down badly, Miriam. I had no alternative — if you can run home whenever you hear a gunshot sound in the township! Master and I have decided that it would be best if you stay home. Now let me pay you your month's wages. I have decided to deduct from your money the cost of the figurine you smashed. Is that okay, Miriam?'

'Yes, Madam. And my reference? I will have to look for other work. My husband is sick at home as you know,' Miriam pleaded softly.

'I shall post your papers, or you can tell your new employer to phone me.' Madam went inside and soon returned with Miriam's wages. 'Now if you don't mind Miriam, my tea is getting cold.'

Miriam walked away, her shoulders slumped. 'Now that is appreciation for all the work I have done here!' she thought.

She walked through the large kitchen, opened the refrigerator and helped herself to a cooldrink. On the table she saw a tempting cream cake topped with red cherries – Master's favourite nightcap! She cut a slice, then another and another – she could not stop eating. When she had had her fill she cut another large slice and wrapped it up to take home to Amos. She picked all the cherries off the topping and stuffed them into her mouth. Finally, feeling satisfied, she went out into the back yard.

Suddenly she remembered that Madam had a bad habit of accusing her servants of stealing. She had a pen in her handbag and she went back to the kitchen. She took a piece of writing paper from the kitchen cupboard drawer and wrote a message to Madam. 'I ate the cake and enjoyed it, Madam.' She pushed the note into the cream of the leftover cake. On her way out she greeted the new maid. 'Poor girl,' she said to herself.

As she walked down the avenue she felt good – even a little happy. 'How foolish can one get! Why should I feel this way over a piece of cake?' she thought. The trees looked even greener than the day before. The birdsongs sounded louder and sweeter. She stopped to open her pay-packet to see how much Madam had taken for the figurine. Counting the money, she discovered that her carelessness had cost her ten rand. She swore to herself!

She decided that she must hurry home now, back to the gunshots and all the chaos. The avenue seemed longer today, or was it perhaps her tiredness? She stopped for a short rest, sitting on an old tree stump. A squirrel ran past her with an acorn in its mouth. As she admired the little creature which scrambled up a huge tree to feed its family, she remembered her family had eaten only mealie meal that morning. She would have to go to the shops on her way through Claremont. The loss of the ten rand for the figurine had set her back financially, but they would manage somehow. She must also buy the daily newspapers for Amos as he was an avid reader. And some fruit and a chocolate for each one! 'But what will I do with Fassie's bar? I will have to keep it until his return,' she said to herself and then, without expecting any answer, 'I wonder where my son is hiding now?'

Suddenly she felt sad as she pictured Amos alone all day,

wobbling around on crutches in the small dark council house. Miriam remembered that he had always bought her fruit and a chocolate bar on his pay-day. She got up from the old tree stump and continued down the road. At the bottom of the hill she turned back and could still see the big house in the distance. She wiped the sweat from her forehead and took one last look at Paradise Road.

Education unrest 1976 uprising

LONGLIVE!

Menán du Plessis

As the combi approached, the youngster on the traffic island lifted a folded paper from the bundle under his arm, shrewdly aware of the lights turning amber up ahead. People peered through the passenger windows, scanning the noon headlines that the child held obligingly close. Dave hunched a shoulder and began to pry out coins from a pocket in his jeans. *Old news, it's the same as the early edition*, he murmured – nonetheless stretching out an arm across Danny's shoulder to offer a first instalment. *Hang on, hang on*, he apologized, trying to drag out another coin.

With a swift flare, sunlight and newsprint were made to collapse under a small elbow – and a skilfully folded paper was handed in through the driver's window. While he waited, the child glanced through the other windows, trying to keep his gaze politely unfocused.

Watching him from inside the combi, Marisa saw his face slowly catch fire with incredulity as he made out the lettering on their yellow T-shirts. One small hand went straight to his mouth, as if to hold back the bright excess of mirth. Then he cried out, with a high-pitched thrill of glee in his voice: *UDF! UDF!*

Viva! Steve called back, while Dave stretched awkwardly half through the window with the remaining coins. Laughing, the people crowded inside the combi raised their fists, offering the casual yet unmistakably militant salutes of comrades. Instantly, the child flashed his own fist high in return. As they pulled away, they heard him belatedly finding words, shouting after them with fierce relish, *Amandla!*

Twisting to watch through the rear window, Marisa gave the response along with the others; while Steve murmured again, with an almost private kind of happiness. *Viva!*

Still looking back, she saw the child dancing on the rapidly receding island; punching repeatedly into the air. *Viva!* she whispered, before straightening round again.

45

Cigarette ash trickled down a page of the newspaper as Dave hunched forward, near-sightedly skimming through the news section. *Anything about the rally?* Danny asked, inclining his head, but keeping his gaze attentively on the road ahead.

No, nothing new. I mean, people know about the restrictions . . .? It was in this morning's Cape Times.

Oh, ja . . . no public address system outside the hall, no gatherings outside and that.

Hmm.

Drawing her shoulders together, Marisa nestled back where she was squeezed in, content to be sharing in this unselfconsciously physical, relaxed closeness. Occasionally through the window she glimpsed delivery trucks, and even small pick-up vans, private *bakkies* – with makeshift wire guards fastened over their windscreens.

Thornton Road someone said, pointing out the narrow street branching off to their left. There was a bend in it only a short way along that helped to obscure the stretching kilometres of its real length. A blind corner – screened by a small stand of wattle bush, still drenched, though it was October already, in a pale, stinking miasma of gold blossom. Nonetheless they were all conscious, briefly hushed, of the killings that had taken place only this week, somewhere down along this road.

They travelled on, passing the junction with Belgravia Road only seconds later. After that lapse into pensiveness they gradually began to reach out again, speaking lightly, without embarrassment.

Ey, it's amazing how much the battle has centred on these two streets.

Ja, someone else said, with the lilting intonation of sudden absorption. *Ja, why is that?*

Several people started to speak at once, attempting to answer; but finally it was left to Dave to carry on describing the number of schools in the area. *And there's also Hewat Training College. . . .*

Yes, Maya added, *right opposite Sinton School, and there's that huge stretch of open ground between them.*

Yes I think that's the point, that's part of it, it's strategic you see: with all those fields, they stretch all the way between Belgravia and Thornton in some parts, so when you've finally got the boere all concentrated in one road – you see . . . (Dave paused briefly, enjoying the vision) *. . . then the lighties can just run straight through to the other side and start re-organizing from there again.*

Well there is a narrow road between Hewat and Sinton, Maya inserted, as if pained by a potential inaccuracy.

True . . . but maybe it's still not as easy for Casspirs to get through as for the lighties – they're on foot remember.

Hmm, Danny commented appreciatively from the front. *It's especially not so easy for the Casspirs when the barricades go up.*

For some time they'd been passing the cramped, shoebox-shaped houses of sub-economic housing schemes. Now the landscape was becoming increasingly bleak and unrelievedly low-horizoned.

Oh, someone said apprehensively, *this is Wetton Road coming up ahead. Is there – hey can anyone see a roadblock, this is where they stopped us last time.*

There was a mild hush inside the combi, though someone cracked a remark about entering the war zone. Yet there were no signs of soldiers or police, and they travelled straight on across the unremarkable sandy verges of the intersection.

Anne-Marie found a boisterous release in chattering now, wanting to finish describing that other experience. *They were actually quite jacked up that time, stopping people from getting in. It was for a funeral we wanted to go to in Crossroads. You know how they have a Buffel, usually they park off at the side of the road, and you see them standing up in it, watching. . . .*

There's always one guy with binoculars. . . .

Those Buffels are big hey, I couldn't believe the first time I actually stood right up next to one.

Hmm . . . but actually have you noticed there doesn't seem to be that much room in them, you've seen – in the newspaper pictures, you always see the troopies really packed in there like sardines, all holding on to that metal side thing; and it's really low, it doesn't even come up to their waists. If you think about it you know, they haven't got much protection, and they're so squashed up there's no room for them to duck, hey. So if they get a stone coming at them!

Or a petrol bomb –

or a bomb, there's actually not much they can do about it; it's

47

no wonder they get into shooting back.

In the distance, way back across the flatlands, receding by the minute, a long, dense row of tall gum trees stretched away into the fading light of the south, in parallel with a fence that was just discernible – surely half imagined only, erected there by some notion of the human mind. There was a cemetery down there; and part of it might be the back of the Kenilworth Racecourse. Probably there was horse-racing on at the moment. It was a Saturday afternoon, after all.

They had slowed down for another intersection, and it seemed they were about to enter a more built-up neighbourhood again. As they crossed, Danny raised one shoulder by way of gesturing, and murmured mildly, *Did you see the lights there – all taken out?*

Marisa twisted sharply, trying to see; but too late.

High overhead there were two kites darting – careering and scything through the wind-scoured air: a paper shape with twin streaming tails; and something that sparkled black as it billowed with light; soaring, pulling higher and higher still above the tenement blocks and the gum-trees and mimosas and the derelict stretches of sand-blown emptiness.

Oh, check, Dave suddenly called out, pointing. And glancing out, they all saw the neatly piled cairns of stones and half-bricks on the sandy verge.

Now these Hanover Park lighties are really organized.

Maya looked up from her knitting needles and stared through the window, one hand resting fretfully on the bright strand of the yarn.

Sherbet I only hope they can see our T-shirts, Dave said mildly. Immediately one of the students in front contorted his body, pressing his torso close up against the window, so that the letters on his T-shirt would be visible. *Pete is a brave man*, someone remarked. Anne-Marie was already holding one of the rally posters squarely up to a side window – also trying hard not to grin, and using both forearms, as though it took great strength to keep the sheet of paper there.

At the civic centre there were already people waiting inside the hall. Someone stepped forward, gave Maya a quick hug; and Danny and Steve were met by a man in khakis who greeted them with arms outstretched. Steve commented on what was evidently a new beard and, faking stern regret, Danny added, *There's just something about you, Rafiek: no matter what you do to yourself you'll be unmistakeable.* Smiling, Rafiek turned to greet more newcomers.

Later it was Rafiek who called for a lull and welcomed the helpers from the various area committees. They still had plenty of work to do, he apologized. Tilting her head, Marisa tried earnestly to pay attention to the words. *Reports we have so far . . .* It was something about extra arrangements – something at the last minute.

. . . the funerals are being attended by anything up to seven thousand people.

Funerals, Marisa thought. . . .

It wasn't only the funeral of the children shot dead in Thornton Road for throwing stones.

There was a man who'd been killed outside a mosque, hit when the police opened fire on a crowd.

Somewhere in the townships there was another man also being buried today: a night watchman who'd died in a blazing shanty. There was a photograph of his young wife – the widow – in the newspaper afterwards: a teenaged woman, with her baby in her arms. Children had come racing into their house, she said: frantic children, eyes bright with the thrill of fear – darting in for shelter; while their grown-up pursuers chased after them first with curses and shot, and then lastly, stingingly, for spite – a hurried can of teargas. She'd tried, she said (and in the newspaper picture her eyes were blurred to an eternal sheen), she'd tried to stifle the fumes with water, but something exploded, and her house was on fire, the blue spirit blazing from a small cooker, wax candles melting in their paper wrapper. Her husband, who was not a young man, had been resting, rigid on their mattress, worn out from his twelve-hour shift of night duty. Even when the zincs began to rattle and slide in the waist-high flames, and she herself was screaming at him, sobbing and gasping – he remained too dulled to stir, unable to help her as she struggled, already keening in grief, to heave his body across her own thin back.

Rafiek paused, spreading out his hands in a gesture that was both generously giving and generously admitting. Despite the short notice, it seemed they had found a minister who was willing to let his church hall be used.... *take up the overflow; of course we can't have people standing outside on the pavement; that would just be an invitation to the police.* Briefly he went into consultation with a woman who stood near him. Like Rafiek she wore khaki – a neat shirt and a pair of slim-fitting trousers; and, perhaps for efficiency, her hair was caught up like a dancer's at the back of her head, in a shining drift.

Afterwards people formed into small clusters, waiting for tasks, while a young woman went around asking if anyone would walk over with her to the second hall. Her name, Marisa picked up, was Vivienne; and she herself was already burdened – awkwardly clasping a large supply of the bright rally posters to her chest. Seeing how some of them were beginning to slip from under her arms, Marisa stepped forward, impulsively offering to take half the pile.

There was an hour and a half before the rally was due to start, but cars were already arriving laden with passengers, and teenagers were beginning to throng on the wide pavements, even in the street itself, despite the traffic cruising up and down. As cars passed, with their hooters braying, the passengers would lean out, clutching on to roof racks, jubilantly contorting themselves as they cheered and raised fists of power. *Viva UDF! Viva ANC! Viva! Viva Mandela!*

Marisa even found herself responding now, though there was still a small trace of self-consciousness in her voice each time she shouted back.

Opposite the centre was an asphalted square, bordered along one perimeter by the yellow brick buildings of a bus terminus. Walking at a relaxed pace, Vivienne and another young woman from the local area led the group towards it. The area seemed too bleak to be a popular place for strolling and meeting, and it was surely too derelict to serve as a parking lot either. Still, there was a small market of a sort near the middle, where an immense blue-gum offered a sparse shade: a few dimly grey striations across the light and the slowly distilled heat of the afternoon. One man had parked his *bakkie* under it and was selling cabbages, onions, potatoes and butter lettuces directly off the back of the small truck. Other hawkers had produce set out on top of plastic crates and wooden boxes. A few women picked

50

shrewdly through the greens in the back of the *bakkie*.

The narrow street on the far side of the square was lined with a row of shops, all with their doors barred up, since it was a Saturday afternoon. One of the large supermarket chains had a branch store here, but the other shops were all probably owned by small businessmen – a halaal butcher, a café, a fish shop.

The volunteers strolled along unhurriedly, walking down the middle of the narrow, sand-washed streets; moving over on to the verges of grey sand only when there were cars approaching. The two people ahead of her were lugging an enormous, sagging burden of clumsily bundled, rolled-up calico. They stumbled frequently, especially in the sand; but somehow they found the breath to mimic their own discomfort. With a little grin of mock annoyance, Marisa hoisted her own bundle of sliding posters; and then suddenly lifted her face to the sky, flooded with the consciousness of being happy.

High overhead – outrageously high – there was a scrap of scarlet stuck against the underside of the whitened sky, pasted there by a child's brilliant strategies with a reel of line and the clear, racing wind.

Viva! she called out huskily. An elderly man on a bicycle waved benignly and worked at the lever of the bell on the handlebars till it gave out a creaking twinge of sound.

Other passers-by were more often suave; coolly intimating by their expressions that they had given these salutes at least a hundred thousand times before. They merely winked back at her, or lazily raised just the flat of a hand.

They turned down a street where the flat-roofed brick houses with their patches of sandy garden now gave way to row after parallel row of municipal tenement blocks, each constructed to an identical plan: three storeys of unfinished brickwork, with metal stairways that jutted from each end of the building, casting bars of rigid shadow across the windows and the sandy ground below. Groups of children stood on a few of the landings, leaning over the railings to stare at the passers-by. Other children, perhaps the bolder ones, came down to the open ground, nimbly ducking under those whipping lines where the bleached and newly rinsed sheets were flaring and cracking in the crisp wind.

Three of them started to jog along beside the group – two

small boys, and a little girl whose gold-brown plaits were weighted with tightly knotted ribbons. Marisa tried winning smiles from them, but their faces remained guardedly expressionless, even when she raised her fist. The little girl's plaits swung to and fro across her shoulders as she carried on running, half walking, half skipping between her two companions.

Reaching St Dominic's, they walked on a short distance, turning in at a small gate behind the generous architecture of the church itself.

Subdued, they put down their various burdens before glancing around – reluctantly, as if they were not ready to face the limitations of the venue. As Rafiek had warned, the hall was not large.

This time it was Shanaaz who took the lead. Lively-eyed, she gave a tiny grimace, acknowledging openly what everyone was thinking, but then started offering a rapid series of suggestions. If they re-arranged the chairs down the sides of the hall, keeping this whole centre part free, then the audience would probably be able to crowd in a bit more; they could sit on the floor. . . . She hesitated. *I mean if they wouldn't mind, or else people will just have to stand.*

And they needed a table for the speakers. *Maybe, what about* . . . Shanaaz looked around the hall again, a sense of purpose in her eyes.

Suddenly energetic, they took no more than a few minutes to break up the existing rows. Light in weight, the plastic chairs separated easily, making only a slight clatter as they raced to stack them – deridingly competitive – five or six high. Once those had been set out, though, in the new configuration, there was disappointingly little else to do. Two helpers had already begun working out a way of stringing up the banner across the back of the stage; and the thin-chested student who stood eagerly by could only hold up a corner of the bulky calico and hope that this was useful.

Shanaaz in the meantime had also wandered up on to the platform, with a quizzical, hopeful expression on her face. Now she and a few other helpers came backing out from the wings, carrying an old wooden table. Vivienne, who was also up there, dusted it absent-mindedly with the flat of her hand once they had positioned it.

A few people were progressing slowly down the length of the hall, sticking up the posters. Marisa stood behind someone, tugging small pieces from a ball of white putty and handing them as they were needed. Looking at the glistening sheets, she registered for the first time that the diagonal flash of colour over the printed words was more than a streak of pure design. *Longlive!* Of course it was a word itself – a cry.

She turned to her partner, surprised. *Longlive ... do you know, what is the response to that?*

Selina used both thumbs to press down the corner of a poster. *I'm not sure what you – How do you mean?*

I mean, what do you answer, when someone shouts that: Longlive. It is a call, isn't it? What do you say back?

A call ... ? Selina seemed doubtful. *I never thought of it like that, I don't know: it's just – I suppose it's the same as a Viva.*

Another hour still stretched ahead of them.

A few people lit cigarettes placidly; took up newspapers that had already been skimmed through once, and carefully unfolded them at arm's length, straightening out creases in the flopping pages.

Someone else suggested a walk. They might as well drift back to the civic hall, take a look at what was happening there.

Teenagers still roved on the pavement outside, pressing together, arms around one another's lean shoulders, laughing, and shouting out catcalls and salutes. Marisa went up to and stood on the periphery of a loose circle round the slim woman in khaki.

Letitia, someone said.

Several busloads were due to be arriving soon from Guguletu. *It's mostly the youth, students, people from the youth congresses ... should be any time now; and there are three more – that is right, Achim, ne? – three buses still to come from Mitchell's Plain also.* The marshals inside had sent out a message to warn that the hall was nearly as full as they would be able to pack it.

Marisa went over to the entrance and edged her way in. Huge brackets of lights were pouring out a mineral glare, saturating the front of the hall with their white heat. She saw Steve, face glistening as he tried to keep a cram of children out of the cordoned area meant for press and television crews. Seeing her, he mimicked an exaggerated state of exhaustion and called out something. This seething noise all around was bewildering. She shook her head. . . . *said it's like trying to marshal the sea*, she heard him shout the second time. She waved, glad to fall back and escape to the outside again.

Just then the first of the hired buses came into sight at the end of the street. Even from a distance they could make out twenty, maybe thirty young men standing on top of the moving bus: braced there somehow on the heavy-duty luggage rack; with both fists raised high in the exultant salutes of victors. There was an awed hiss of admiration from the waiting crowd, and a few nimble teenagers went sprinting down the road to meet the visitors half-way. Escorted by the racing youths, the bus came down the street, travelling very slowly, with a smooth, sustained precision; and now the initial uproar became a chaotic thickness of sheer, unceasing sound. *Amandla! Amandla!* Three or four people at least craned from every window, leaning out to shout *Viva UDF! Viva ANC!* Still more were crowded in behind them, standing in the aisle, crushed in, singing. With immense care the driver brought the bus up alongside. As the brakes began dragging the men on the roof stood firm, poised to withstand the coursing through their bodies of the bus's last momentum; but the instant the wave had passed, they moved forward, to spring directly into the vigorous steps of a dance.

The singing of the new arrivals was taken up by the crowd on the pavement; and now scores of young people came surging out, abandoning the safety of the hall to see the comrades arriving. And as if to reciprocate, the young men on the roof came clambering down, leaping to the pavement and then, hardly pausing to recover, lithely moving forward, straight back into the fluid, powerful rhythm. Each one carried on performing. determinedly untiring, until the entire company had regrouped on the ground: and even then, though their faces were bright with sweat, they refused to interrupt the dance, until the applause had become such a storm that finally no one could hear any more words of the song.

Marshals were beginning to move around the edges of the crowd, mildly trying to direct people back into the hall.

The driver of the bus had climbed out to open the door for his passengers. Each one on reaching the top step paused for a second to raise a fist, before springing down to follow the others who were on their way in, slowly running, singing as they made for the entrance, and raising fists.

Another bus pulled up; and shortly afterwards three more turned into the street, one behind the other: all of them travelling with the same cautiously lumbering slowness; all of them carrying at least a hundred, perhaps a hundred and fifty passengers precariously leaning out, and singing.

Marisa saw Penny and Selina emerging from the hall and wandered over to join them. They should probably be heading back to St Dominic's.

Entered this second time, the hall no longer seemed so disappointing. The light in the place was no longer the timid, imperceptible colour of dust, but warmly alive with a shimmering of red and gold. The posters, for one thing, now formed a continuous frieze around the walls; and someone had draped the speaker's table with lengths of black and red jersey cloth. There was even a bowl of flowers gracing the platform – one of the pair originally meant for the civic hall.

Suspended right across the back of the stage, the giant sail of calico was impressive as a backdrop. It hardly mattered that it was an old one, dating from the launch of the Front – two years back. Nowadays, the banners were certainly much finer: massive compositions, painted on to the fabric with a quiet, almost tender regard for craft, even when it came to lettering, or adding a faint trace of colour. Nonetheless, this early design had a power of its own, with its strung-out, painted scene of people on the march behind the banner of the UDF, gathering strength along their route from tiny figures the artists had depicted streaming up to join the moving column.

It was not long before the first cheering, impetuous crowd of students came bursting in, singing as they ran in steadily from the bus that had driven up outside. The front-runners kept on moving once they were indoors, sweeping down to the edge of the stage before they veered around and began to dance, while one of them skirted around to the steps at the side and took the stage.

Briefly the solo artist danced up there for everyone, rapturously skilful, delighting in their delight in him. The singing even fell away for a time, as people breathed harder, hissing involuntarily, keeping their elbows dipping backwards and forwards, their feet moving and stamping, lurching sideways. All the while they kept their eyes on the stage performer: that one who danced with no sign of effort, face shining in gratitude, embodying the final achievement of each one's own energetic, ceaseless striving.

Slowly the hall filled, as bus after bus pulled up outside. People continued to dance, persistent in their enthusiasm.

A few of the more experienced marshals were clustered casually near the steps, speaking to new arrivals; now and then looking out across the rapidly crowding-in audience. They were mostly quite young, wearing jeans or khaki slacks, bright T-shirts with slogans, anoraks, Lebanese scarves. Unsure of her own role now, Marisa stood hovering near the stage, beating her hands together softy, wistfully keeping the rhythm.

No one seemed particularly impatient for the rally to begin. Every now and then someone would break through the crowd and find a way up to the platform, where a round of handshakes, embraces, waves, small conversations would occur.

One of these was a woman who arrived with a young girl at her side. Marisa saw how a marshal in a yellow T-shirt went ahead of her, hands clasped high to form a kind of human prow as he barged a way slowly through the dancing crowd for them. After she'd been helped up she was guided to a seat at the speakers' tables, while another marshal darted away to fetch a chair for the child. Recovering her breath, the woman continued chattering warmly, Touching someone's hand or cheek, smiling, head bobbing, turning anxiously to greet a friend she'd not seen earlier.

After some time a young man stepped to the foot of the stage and held up both hands, keeping them patiently raised until he was granted an interlude of quiet.

He spoke in Xhosa first: head slightly inclined, hands lightly held out to his audience. If you looked only at his relaxed stance and the kindly, attentive expression, you might have taken him for a listener rather than a speaker. Wondering who he was, Marisa tried to make out the lettering on his dark T-shirt. The logo showed four hands interclasped to form a ring of solidarity, with a motto below it: An injury to one is an injury to all.

Someone from a trade union, probably. Switching to English, he explained the same thing over again: they were still trying to organize a sound system. People had gone to fetch microphones, loudspeakers. *In the meantime* – he smiled warmly . . . *you can carry on dancing*.

The audience took him at his word.

Faces were now beginning to glitter, and T-shirts steadily darkened, clinging damply to gleaming chests and shoulders. *Phantsi Botha, phantsi, phantsi*, a group chanted in mirth, using both hands to pantomime a sturdy pushing downward; pretending to add the full weight of their bodies slowly, shimmying low as they forced some imaginary creature down to the ground. The dancers' eyes were shedding brightness by the time they had wriggled themselves up straight again, to cheering whistles and shouts of applause.

For a while the singing changed into a long round of chants, which still maintained the rhythm of a dance – with the warm, thudding percussion of whistle-bursts, handclaps, and stamping.

They had been waiting now for at least half an hour. At least. And maybe there were two thousand people, or two and a half . . . even three thousand, stiffly packed. All these shimmering faces.

Copies of a newspaper came around, passed on overhead from hand to hand; and now that they had something to study, there were many who chose to begin slowly threading their way from the floor, in search of seats.

Waving the folded tabloid, a woman shooed off three children who'd wrested occupation of a chair. Marisa glimpsed the masthead on someone else's copy, and recognized the name of the community paper.

Only a small group in the middle of the crush still seriously persisted in dancing. Shyly, still tentatively offering her own quiet hand-clapping as she danced, Marisa tried to draw closer. The dancers were holding up the spread sheets of the newspaper – slowly revolving to display the headline. It was the first time she'd properly seen. CHILDREN KILLED. As if to ensure that no one would fail to see, the dancers kept the pages high, occasionally resting, allowing them to dip, but then lifting them again, with an almost sombrely determined power of endurance, still moving, shifting round.

A few singers in the circle were repeating a single phrase over and over – establishing it, almost, as the first inspiration for a song.

Silesa – the line came again.

'We read', it meant. Yet there was something missing still: surely the sentence was unfinished.

Silesa –

Nonetheless – simply as music, the small fragment of song was already, in itself, an answer of a sort . . . or perhaps a kind of a ground.

One after another, various singers offered further lines, experimentally: more intricate lyrics, melodically woven over the steadily repeated response.

Silesa – the dancers chanted again, assuredly, as if encouraging the soloists.

To find words for the knowledge that children had been killed. Shot dead in a suburban street, for throwing stones.

It was very hot in the hall; people could hardly breathe. The necessary lyrics refused to be found.

The dancers persisted, though small frowns were beginning to flicker across faces. It should have been unthinkable . . . yet it seemed their power of endurance might be threatening to fail.

At last Rafiek arrived, arms grappled round a cumbersome, obviously heavy loudspeaker. He was followed up on to the stage by a group of teenagers carrying the rest of the equipment. Leaving it to them to set up, he came across to a young man sitting behind the speakers' table. A youth, really: slim build, and a fragile, still sparse growth of beard.

After a glance up at Rafiek, he gave a nod and got to his feet, gatherine a few papers from the table in front of him.

The man in the trade union T-shirt was already standing relaxedly behind one of the microphones, waiting to act as interpreter. He glanced back constantly at the teenagers, occasionally tapping the microphone in response to requests from them.

The student had finished his appeal for unity, and now the next speaker prepared himself while the interpreter was busy with the introduction.

A copy of the previous day's *Weekly Mail* went on to the table nearby, as if to be kept within reach.

When the interpreter turned to him, Comrade X took a vigorous step forward and immediately began a long series of energetic calls, backing up each one with a firm punch into the air. Ardently, the crowd came back each time, shouting the appropriate responses. *Ngawethu!*

Amandla! Ngawethu! Ngawethu! Amandla!

A person's thoughts could begin to drift freely through the impassioned uproar.

Inkululeko! Ngoku! Ngoku! Inkululeko! Mayibuye! iAfrika!

Somehow in the way it was structured, the chanting came close to poetry.

Not ordinary poetry, she thought. More like that strong kind out of the old Greek dramas, that had to be acted out on the hot sand – in stone theatres open to the drifting light, the blowing scent of resin, the shadows of clouds. There were terms she half-remembered. Strophe, and antistrophe.

Viva UDF! Viva! Viva UDF! Viva!

Eventually X signalled that he wanted to begin. *Comrades –* he said: and after a quick glance at him, the interpreter followed with the Xhosa, also holding a hand high in a mild request for attention. *Maqabane –*

X continued, *The government is trying to divide us –* The moment his voice implied an interim cadence, the interpreter came in with the paraphrase. And while the interpreter was uttering the last soft syllable of the Xhosa, X took back the platform to deliver another phrase in English.

The government comes into our townships – Marisa made out the word *amabhulu* in the Xhosa parallel. She knew it meant the boere; which meant the Afrikaners, really – or the police. Or nowadays (someone had told her) it could even mean all whites in general.

. . . tell us through their loudspeakers – X went into a little burlesque, making a funnel with his hand to mimic a man using a loudhailer. The audience chuckled, perhaps in recognition.

They try to tell us that the people who say the troops must get out of the townships – Now that he was sure of his audience X's strong face began to gleam with the warm, generous confidence of someone who delighted in his own capacity to give – in words, as well as in actions. *– that those people are our enemies.*

There was a word in the Xhosa that sounded like 'location'.

But we know who our enemies are —

The enemies are the people who are shooting at our children —

The ones who come with guns, in their Casspirs.

Comrades, we are meeting today —

We are remembering many comrades who have died.

Today — today the people have buried some of these comrades.

But despite their deaths, in spite of these deaths, the people — we who are the people — are united: nothing can destroy our unity, Comrades: their bullets will not destroy our unity; their teargas will not destroy our unity. . . .

X was exultant now, somehow conveying more eagerness, greater power with each phrase: *. . . not even when they come with their Casspirs. . . .*

There was a glinting of teeth, a shine in people's eyes, making it clear that an outbreak of cheering and laughter was imminent.

The government will never destroy the unity of the people now.

On impulse he stepped forward, willingly interrupting the rhythmic flow of his own phrases to shout out, *Viva!*

The cry gave the audience their chance to shout back, and spontaneously a few teenagers added further calls, leading the rest into another protracted round of chanting: as if they were reluctant to end this direct involvement along with X in the making of the speech.

Inkululeko! Ngoku! came the reply.

Freedom now. Marisa felt her earlier fatigue disappearing. With a sudden spirited sense of release she joined in the next response — wanting (for the first time actively wanting) to be at one with the multitude in shouting out this word, *Inkululeko!* Wasn't that what ectasy meant? A standing outside. Not apart from the masses, but a part of; standing outside oneself — that was the whole point.

A luta! Continua! Victoria! È certa!

It was several moments before X could continue and when he did speak again, it was in a quieter mood.

I want to talk about two comrades. One is a comrade — an old comrade — who died this week — He paused for the interpreter, glancing sideways with a flickeringly rueful smile, as though he had momentarily lost his sense of the rhythm. But he seemed to recover as soon as he'd finished the last phrase: – *overseas in Havana: that's the capital city of Cuba – another country . . . across the sea.* With a bold sweep of one arm, he indicated how remote that other country was. The audience was giving him their fullest concentration now.

Just detectably, X stepped up the pace.

The name of this comrade . . .

. . . Igama lakhe bengu Aliks la Guma.

Now, most of us have never even heard this comrade's name: that's because the government of this country has kept us from knowing about him, and from reading his books. But he was one of this country's greatest writers. Now what the government did to him – they put him under house arrest. He couldn't go out of his own house for five years, Comrades.

There were low whistles of dismay, and people shook their heads slowly, sympathetically exclaiming. *So then in the end he had to leave this country, to take up the struggle . . . .* As he waited for the final cadence of the Xhosa phrase X pointed, using the sweep of his whole arm, until the beat came again and he could finish: . . . *from outside.* Again the gesture made it plain that 'outside' was somewhere almost fantastically remote, hidden away on the other side of the planet's vast, curving surface. *And when he died, he was the representative for the ANC, he stood for the ANC in Cuba.*

As if trying to head off an imminent uproar, X went on hurriedly: *One day, when we have a people's government, and the people decide what we will teach, and what we will read, and what we will study – then we will read his books, the books of this comrade, and his name also will not die.*

Dancing and stamping, people raised their fists – both fists – and chanted steadily, shouting out with a heartbreaking vibrancy of determination, *Viva Alek la Guma! Viva! Longlive la Guma! Longlive! Longlive! Longlive!*

It was a while before X could resume. Eventually, though, he took the microphone again, raising one hand in a gently steadying gesture as if to warn that his next words would also be serious.

There's another comrade we are thinking about today. He died yesterday – in Pretoria – where he was put to death by the

61

government: our comrade Benjamin Moloise.

The audience grew very still.

We all know his name I think. We know why the government hanged him: for his part in the struggle.

But he was very strong before he died. And he left a message for us, comrades: he wrote a poem . . . that is – some words, a message. In this poem he says that he was proud to die: he was not afraid.

X reached for the folded *Weekly Mail*. Making it clear that he was quoting from it, he read out carefully:

I am proud to be what I am;
I am proud to give my life:
My one life.

For the first time the interpreter hesitated before responding at the end of each phrase; and when – after consideration – he delivered Moloise's lines in Xhosa, he spoke them carefully, and quietly.

People sat in stillness, many keeping their heads bowed, though others stared forward with the blinded, momentarily rigid expressions of grief. A woman tried to veil her face with her hand, but the fingers strayed listlessly.

Someone softly, waveringly, started to sing.

Thina sizwe . . .

And a few of the men came in, offering the same words, *Thina sizwe.*

> *. . . esimnyama*

but in a slower, deeper melody.

> *. . . esimnyama*

Gradually the entire audience took up the elusive, attenuated hymn. We, the black nation. . . . Clenched fists remained steadily raised, but often only to shoulder height, as though the gesture had no anger in it now, but only the aching sense of solidarity.

Abantwana . . .

> *Abantwana*
> *. . . beAfrika*
> *beAfrika*

Many kept their heads bowed as the gentle anthem drifted on:

Elathatwa . . .

taken away

> *. . . ngamabhulu*

by the boers
sung with a tender slowness – each of the two melodies drawn
out and lingered over in its turn,
   Mabayeke umhlaba wethu
   Let it come back to us –
      our land
         umhlaba wethu
until it was entirely mingled with the other.

The interpreter was introducing the woman who'd brought the
young girl with her on to the platform.

There was something comforting about the simple, ordinary
solidity of Auntie Y's physical appearance. When she stood up
you saw how her plump feet were swollen over the sides of her
old, comfortably worn-in shoes; and yet her face suggested a
kind of brisk contentment. As she waited she tried to straighten
the lengths of cloth on the table, unceremoniously pushing aside
the bowl of silk flowers, with its impromptu addition of spilling
wattle leaves.

Her face brightened to a deep gold as she began to speak.

Out of urgency, perhaps, her voice had a streak of shrillness to
it. After a few moments, the audience began glancing around,
obviously working hard to restrain their embarrassment at the
blithe stream of high-pitched, sharp vowels.

Even if you could not catch everything she said, there was no
mistaking that Y spoke the Afrikaans of the upcountry farming
districts. Frowning slightly, the interpreter took a half step
forward and raised a hand in mild admonition. *Come,
Comrades, come; let us hear what Auntie Y has to say.*
Immediately responsive, people smoothed away the grins and
settled themselves to listen.

Y did not seem to have noticed the brief hints of ridicule.
Unreflectingly perhaps, she merely assumed her right to speak as
she had always spoken. Catching her breath, she repeated her
eager demand that parents should stand united together with
their children.

The young girl kept her face lowered; sitting with her hands
folded meekly in the lap of her dress.

Gradually Y's unflinchingly strident sentences became compelling. The accent seemed to matter less and less, and finally

63

became unnoticeable. *Die hele gemeenskap – the whole community must stand united in its demand for the troops to get out of the townships.*

After a burst of applause, the interpreter took the chance to offer a résumé in Xhosa. Y was switching constantly between English and Afrikaans, but the rapidity of her speech meant there were few natural breaks for translation into the third language. Perhaps in compensation for the brevity of the Xhosa version, the interpreter offered a shout of *Amandla!* and the response came back with an edge of aggressive satisfaction to it.

Y drew the young girl to her feet now, encouraging her to stand near the microphone. As she started to speak again, she gently took the child by the wrist and helped her to raise her arm. Although the child's face had a softly radiant quality still, her expression was impassive. Obediently she kept her hand raised.

I brought this little girlie with me today. I'm from Worcester, now, and she's only one of the children living in my street. Only . . . and she's now only eleven years old.[1]

Then it wasn't Y's own child. A neighbour's daughter.

Well, I brought her with because I want . . . I brought her so that you can see for yourselves.

Y was tugging gently at the child's arm again, as if she wanted her to do something; perhaps to step forward. *You can see for yourselves what they did.*

There was a faint hiss of indrawn breath from the crowd.

That was when she saw the child's hand: the pitiful stumps where the fingers had been.

She turned away, trying to bury her face against the shoulder of the woman nearest her, who was whispering something.

And she's only one, Y continued, a bitter clarity in her eyes. She had to raise her voice to be heard now above the steady murmurs of distress.

There's also another child – and I'm telling you I'm only talking about the children I know personally. She broke off to give her attention briefly to the child, who had quietly reseated herself. Re-organizing, Y put an arm around the small shoulders

[1] Auntie Y's speech has been translated into English.

64

that were now slightly drawn up and tense under the crisp white ruffles of broderie anglaise.

And now this other child that I know is also a girl – twelve years old.

No, Marisa thought, feeling a small, sudden tightness of rebellion in her throat. Whatever it is, please, don't make us hear any more.

And when she came back from the hospital –

Y halted, and for a moment looked unexpectedly helpless, as if for once she could not find words. With that stricken look still in her eyes, she carried on bravely nonetheless, in the only way she could; attempting to describe what had happened to the other little girl.

There was no one who failed to understand when Y indicated her right arm from the shoulder downward – and used a brief, unambiguous gesture to convey the sense of a severance.

A few women began to wail, some with such intensity that they seemed to be screaming.

Then there was a surge, and people were on their feet, shouting out over and over, hoarsely, struggling to find relief. Even if any translation had been needed, words would have been trampled over, broken apart in this chaos. The groans of pity kept on; the shouting becoming voice-tearing in its volume, as people seemed to try out every conceivable human sound for a power of expression that might rise beyond and outlive this, finding some reason or meaning for it.

Rafiek had just driven up, and was waiting, ready to give them a lift back to the civic hall. The place was as clean now as they were going to get it, everyone acknowledged dispiritedly. Shanaaz bent down to pick up an overlooked cigarette butt.

The posters had come down almost within minutes of the rally's ending, seized from the walls as prizes. The hall was already virtually deserted when Vivienne came across a small boy still inside. He was kneeling reverently, she said, in front of a chair: using the plastic seat as a surface where he could fold his two captured posters with an earnest perfectionism.

Outside, they were surprised to find it nearly dusk. Already misty, the light hung wavering between amber and grey above the wastes of cold-shadowed sand. People had begun turning on lights in the apartments, and there were pale squares of yellow set into the solid regions of darkness formed by the tenement blocks.

The vinyl of the car seat was chilly, rather clammy, when they climbed in and shifted along, crowding in.

Rafiek had the engine already running when someone peering back saw Matthew loping up from out of the semi-darkness. The instant he reached them, he leaned down to the window: *You people ready to leave? I was just coming across to see if you needed any more help clearing up.* Swinging himself quickly in and closing the door, he added, *There's a bit of trouble back there. Rafiek can we go then?* And he leaned back for a second. In the front seat, Charmaine twisted round to ask what was happening.

Okay hang on I just need a smoke, has anyone . . . ? Someone passed him a lit cigarette and he took a deep, relieved draw on it. His face was startlingly pale – burning white. Hurriedly he leaned forward again: *No Rafiek, Rafiek – rather go straight on, we can't go back that way now. There's shooting going on. We'll just have to take a turn round the block.*

Clearly relieved they were under way, he rested his hands loosely on his jutting knees. *People are trying to get into Checkers now.* Casually, he cursed. *I nearly, as I was on my way here, I was coming across – you know that area past the shop –*

They sat forward, listening intently.

The crowd are just going wild now, he went on, with a kind of disbelieving, light acerbity. *I heard these shots – really loud, like, just past my head: then I saw it was this security guard, shooting straight at me.*

What with a shot gun –

No no he just had a handgun. You always see these guys wearing holsters. He cursed again, lightly; shaking his head with a faint grin. *But it's bullets.*

There was a slight, rapid tremor in his hands. His whole body must still be surcharged with the energy of crisis. Marisa felt a scurry of nervousness, but sharply dismissed it. What in hell, at least they were all together.

Okay – we, look we've already decided back at the civic we're not even going to try and marshall it. The meeting was already over when these people started pulling together outside the hall again – I mean it's actually beyond our control now. We're still sticking around, clearing up, but basically we've finished – we were just waiting for you to finish up here.

Ja, Rafiek murmured, obviously worried, but concentrating firmly on his driving.

Someone cursed again softly. *Just what we don't need.*

Oh hell ja.

. . . what it's going to look like in the newspapers: UDF rally ends in a riot.

They were nearing the square now surely. The twilight had been deepening with each passing second, and the last traces of lilac had already died away into smudged ash and shadow. Angrily Marisa smothered a sense of frustrated will. Peering out like the others she made out buildings that were half familiar now; and – unmistakeably, even in the dimness – there was the pale, glistening trunk of the giant blue-gum. Matthew wound the window down, and across the chilly, sparkling air they heard the thrilled shouting, from the edge of the night. As Rafiek drove cautiously past, they saw a rack of vivid amber shimmering up into the darkness.

Do you think they're going to torch the place? someone said uneasily.

They could see a vague blur of movement around the front of the department store: figures jumping up and down, people running up.

As soon as Rafiek had pulled up outside the hall, they bundled out, gathering their things, already searching the dusk for familiar faces. Marisa lingered, not even certain what it was she still wanted – other, perhaps, than to say goodbye with proper care. Rafiek turned slightly, spreading one arm along the back of the passenger seat. *There really is nothing more you can do,* he said quietly. *Our . . . I think our local committee will be staying around to keep an eye on things.*

Bending her head, she said goodbye and then climbed out hurriedly, trying to give him a last smile. He's very kind, she thought.

Steve was standing under a streetlight; and she caught sight next of Danny – the familar bushy beard, mild dark eyes. Swiftly she went up to join them; and found that the others were here as well – faces serious, with hair sticky and tangled over pale

67

foreheads. Shivering in her thin cotton T-shirt, she moved close to Steve. Somewhere a hooter was blaring incessantly. *Stupid moron*, she thought, wishing they were out of this alien place.

From across the square they heard a series of fast, hard reports. She and Maya turned sharply, helplessly looking to Danny – who anticipated the question. *No, it's I think it's just stones, bricks*, he said. *They're trying to break down the door. . . .*

Fiercely, Marisa remembered kites.

Trying to stop shivering, she concentrated on the thought of a child's energetically burning, bitter delight in tearing over the sandy wastelands. She smiled, and forced herself to carry on dreaming.

Danny patted her lightly on the arm. *You coming in the combi, or else there's also – no, Aviva's left already, okay come get in.*

At last they were on the road.

Dave leaned back tiredly against the seat. *It's unbelievable that the boere haven't pulled in yet.*

Ja, we hardly saw them all day. They've been keeping a low profile.

Danny called back, *Well frankly I think they were probably wise to. I don't know what it was like at St Dom's, but like at the civic hall, I tell you the mood sometimes. . . .*

As they headed on to the freeway, finally leaving the area, they still stared back, faces close to the mirroring windows, struggling to see beyond the coppery light of reflection on the inside, and the darkness pressing up against the cold outer surface of the glass.

They all glimpsed the three slender youths racing along the pavement with their heads down, hands gripped on to billowing anoraks. Moving in the direction of the action, they took long, easy strides – running with a strange kind of carefulness. A streetlight flooded them briefly in a stark blaze of shadows. Inside the bottle that one of them was carrying, something kept dipping and levelling.

Steve continued to peer out into the darkness for a long time. He looked pale. Maybe he was tired, Marisa thought. She was waiting for him to whisper *Viva*.

Women leaders
Dedicated to Mrs Winnie Mandela and all South Africa's women leaders

A NOTION
OF SISTERHOOD

Bernadette Mosala

'Jean, my spencer vest is not quite dry yet and I suspect I am catching the flu. Can I borrow yours till tomorrow please?'

'Okay Tizzy, it's in the chest of drawers; and do be careful – look after yourself. This flu in the air is quite a killer you know.'

'I don't know what's happening to me Jeanie but I really feel bad.'

It was a cold winter morning in Room 208 at Barnato Hall, one of the halls of residence at the University of the Witwatersrand in Johannesburg. The two young women, Jean Finney and Tizzy Khumalo, were room-mates. They were both in their second year in the Faculty of Social Science. They had lived together from the time of their arrival at the university. Their relationship was a remarkable one because, unlike other room-mates, they had really stuck together.

The circumstances surrounding their closeness were not pleasant. It was a few weeks after the university term had started. There was a notice on the bulletin board that announced that all black students had been refused ministerial approval to study at a white university and as such had to leave the university campus within 72 hours. As would have been expected, after a mass meeting the whole student body came out in protest against the announcement. The meeting had further moved that no black student should leave. White students were urged to room-in with them. The motion was unanimously adopted. It was at that point that Jean invited Tizzy to share her room, and Tizzy agreed. They had not known each other from a bar of soap. Tizzy was overwhelmed by Jean's gesture to say the least. In addition to the anger of the protestors and her nervousness at being at the university, her greatest worry was the idea of living with a white so closely – day in and day out. However, her innate determination came to her rescue, so that within a comparatively short time they were getting on very well together, and from then on they never looked back.

Tizzy's home was in Soweto with the rest of her family. She was a wiry and intense girl who had had to remember all the time that she must fight all the way if she was to be anything. The spirit of determination that pervaded her outlook on life had given her a slight scowl on her forehead that belied her very genial disposition which was the hallmark of her family.

Jean came from Sandton in the northern suburbs of the city. Her family were comfortably off. That was borne out by the fact that their room had a little fridge, a colour television set and a pioneer music centre. They used these at will, and really had a good time together. Jean had an athletic figure. She loved sport and squash in particular. She displayed a beautiful sunburn which was the result of the many hours she spent on the outdoors squash courts. In the protected environment of Wits, over the two years the two young women had become somewhat oblivious to what went on beyond the gates of the university.

'Tizzy, it's seven-thirty already, hurry up, you know how fussy Mrs Goldstein is about coming late to her lectures,' urged Jean who was already at the door with her bag.

'Where are the disprins that we had? I need to take two now to keep my temperature down.'

'Aren't they there on the lamp-stand? That's where I saw them last; and that was two days ago. Do take your scarf – there's an icy breeze for sicklings.'

Tizzy did not respond to the last jab from Jean. She was frantically trying to find the tablets. Eventually she found them on the carpet behind the lamp-stand. By then Jean was out on the little street that led up to the Social Science block.

'Did you take the keys Jeanie?' shouted Tizzy just before she pulled the door behind her.

'Yeh, I've got them,' Jean responded, dangling them up in the air for Tizzy to see.

At the end of lectures Tizzy decided to stay in bed with the hope of sweating out the flu. During the afternoon Jean had gone out to play squash in the gymnasium. She really loved the game

71

so much that nothing could keep her from it even for a day. She came back to have a quick shower before going to the students' refectory for supper.

'Tizzy, how is it – are you still alive mate?'

'Ya – it's okay,' mumbled Tizzy from under the blankets. 'What time is it there?'

'6 o'clock, chum!'

Tizzy just gave one long moan of regret. It was time for her to get up for supper too. The dining hall was three blocks away and they were not supposed to take food into their rooms. Sick students were expected to go to the sick bay where facilities for feeding them were available. But who wanted to see herself in the sick bay?

When Jean heard her groan like she did, she tried to cheer her up: 'Don't you worry, Tiz, its a matter of a few months now that we are in this boarding school, then we'll be out and living like adults.'

'What are you talking about?' blurted Tizzy from under the blankets. Her main preoccupation was how to avoid leaving her warm bed and still get her supper.

'Have you forgotten? In three months' time we shall be living in a commune where everything will be under one roof: f-o-o-d, f-r-i-ends, bedrooms. Super – don't you think?'

By then Tizzy was crawling out of bed. 'You're right. That will be fine. How can one not catch the flu? One moment you're in a warm room, the next you're walking in the cold.' She sat on the bed with all the blankets wrapped around her. Eventually she got ready to go to the dining room.

In their last year, they left Barnato Hall for a commune in Trematon Place in Parktown. The house had eight young adults living in it. Their arrival raised the number to ten. One bedroom had become available when the young man who had occupied it had decided to leave the country because he did not want to do military service. They were very happy with the room, the company, and the location of the house. It was easily within walking distance of the university. In fact, having settled in, Tizzy one night asked, 'Tell me Jean, why didn't we think of this idea earlier? Fancy us inflicting all the drab campus life on ourselves for two years!'

'I dunno, I suppose there is substance in what they say –

'things will always happen at their right time' – heard about that one?'

'Get lost, with your cheap philosophy. Who are you trying to impress? Not me.'

'You are disgusting. You can't even credit a person when she makes a real effort to be erudite.'

They both laughed.

That August, Jean and Tizzy decided to attend a National Women's Conference in Grahamstown to mark the end of the International Women's Year. As usual the great majority of the participants were white women. There was, however, a fair sprinkling of black women other than Tizzy Khumalo, although nearly all could have been either her mother or her granny.

Both young women were enthusiastic about the status and the size of the conference until the mayoress gave her official opening address. She dwelt very heavily on the importance of the family to the community:

'Ladies, I am very delighted that I have been asked to officially open this historic conference. I am even more delighted that the conference has such a strong focus on the family. Ladies, it is common knowledge that the family is the nucleus of society and that women have a crucial role to play in its well-being. We are called upon to make sure that our families keep together in these trying times when there are so many pressures and influences that threaten to pull it apart. We must stand close to our husbands as they strive to build the nation and our land. Nothing must ever be allowed to break family life.'

Tizzy was amazed and angered by her arguments. During tea-break she went up to the mayoress, who was at the time surrounded by white women, both English- and Afrikaans-speaking, who were singing praises to her paper. She stood there trapped in her tradition and culture. How could she interrupt her elders? 'It's never done,' the little voice of her upbringing told her. She felt very young. Yes, she was scared and nervous. Her lips went dry and she kept licking them. Her hands were sweating. She secretly stole a glance at them. She saw the tiny heads of sweat glistening in the feeble winter sun. Casually she put her hands on her buttocks pretending to be as relaxed as ever, although her intention was to dry them on the brown corduroy jeans she was wearing.

Eventually the mayoress got a chance to chip in after that avalanche of praises. 'Come on now ladies, you're too nice to me. I am certain anyone of you could do even better. But I thank you for your generosity.'

At that point she was given a round of applause by the little group that had formed around her. When it died down, Tizzy seized the opportunity to address her. After her first few words the little group seemed to hold their breath in consternation.

'Mrs Mayor or is it Mayoress? Pardon my ignorance please. Anyway I have a question there wasn't time to ask after the lecture. When you speak of 'family' what exactly do you mean in a migrant situation? The point I want to make is, if the husband lives in a single-sex hostel in Cape Town and the wife and children are in Zwelitsha in the Ciskei – where is family in that situation?'

'Listen my dear, I am not a politician and I believe this is not a political conference either, neh?'

But Tizzy was not going to be put off easily. 'Mayoress, let me put it another way then. When you and your family sit around your table and enjoy family life, does it ever occur to you that the men in the single-sex hostel, whose wives are in the rural areas, need to enjoy the same kind of family warmth? And that in fact it is their right, although we know that only for the white section of the population of this land is it a *legal* right?'

Tizzy could hardly finish the question before some white women whisked the mayoress away. This little incident caused a bit of a stir. Tizzy was left on her own – half scared, half happy with herself that she had spoken, until Jean came and took her away from the glare of the crowd. She put her arm around her and said quietly, 'Well done Tizzy, I'm proud of you.'

'Thanks Jean.'

From that time Tizzy seemed to carry a spotlight around her. At every session white women seemed to look out for her. Many times she would catch two or three pointing at her while speaking in subdued voices. During a very interesting session that afternoon, Jean tiptoed up to Tizzy and whispered to her to leave the debate at once. She led her out of the conference hall, right out of the foyer even. This felt very strange to Tizzy.

'Hey, what's up; what's all this?' she asked.

'Let's go and sit over there for a while.' Jean pointed at an oleander that was in full pink bloom.

'Look Jean, I don't want to go there; I want to go back into the hall, what's wrong with you?'

'You need to hear this.'

'Must it be *now*?'

'In fact even *before now*. Listen. I was in the loo when a small group of women came and stopped at the wash area. They were speaking Afrikaans in whispers, but the anger in their voices kept them high enough for me to hear what they said.'

'What has that got to do with me?'

'Shhh – please listen. It's you they were talking about. Looks like there is a plot to lynch you tonight. I suppose it has something to do with what you said to the mayoress. They even know that you are in room 24.'

'Are you serious?'

'Why do you think I'm here? Now listen, tonight we are going to swop rooms. You sleep in mine and I'll sleep in yours.'

'And what if you get hurt for my sake? No, I won't do that. Moreover it has a smack of cowardice. *I* addressed the mayoress and it is *I* who will bear the consequences, Jean.'

'No Tizzy, you listen to me. You are going to do as I say and that's it. I know they mean it. It was in their tone and above all they are the executive of the *Vrouè Federasie* – those are the hard Afrikaner women, make no mistake about that. Let's go back now.'

Tizzy did not quite know what was happening to her. She wanted to meet these stubborn women and have it out with them. But on the other hand she felt she should respect her friend's judgment.

That night things happened according to Jean's plan. In the dead of night, room 24 was invaded. Jean had deliberately covered her head. The 'invaders' were armed with all kinds of pain-inflicting instruments. They had luggage straps, broomsticks, high-heeled shoes, wooden coat-hangers, pins, and even pillows. As soon as they got in, they surrounded the bed and began to attack the sleeper. This threw Jean into another level of shock – she had thought there would be a discussion before the lambasting, and she had hoped for a slim chance of talking them out of it.

Now she feared for her life. For the first time she experienced what it was like to be the butt of the blind anger of white people. The physical pain they were inflicting was nothing compared to her emotional one. She began to scream from under the blankets, and that seemed to spur them on. Tizzy in room 25 heard the screams and the blows. How could she sleep, when she knew her friend's life was in danger for her sake? She rushed out into room 24 where she found a ghastly sight. A moment before she walked in, Jean had thrown off the blankets and was staring at a group of women. One arm was covering her head in an effort to protect it from the blows that were raining on her. When Tizzy walked in, quite a number of arms were poised to deliver blows, but had somehow got frozen in mid-air. Their eyes were almost popping out of their sockets and their faces white with shock at the realisation that they had been beating a white woman.

In the frozen silence, Tizzy spoke. 'Jean, are you all right?'

'I don't know.'

After this, one of the 'invaders' asked in Afrikaans, '*Wat is hierdie kamer se nommer dan*?' (What is this room's number then?)

'Why do you ask?' Tizzy responded.

'*Waar slaap jy*?' (Where do *you* sleep?)

'Why?' Jean intervened. 'Is it any business of yours where she sleeps? I think I would like to lay a charge of common assault right now.'

There was a shuffle of feet in an attempt to escape, but Tizzy had planted herself in the doorway and had no intention of letting anyone out. Six white women all bunched up at the door. When they realised Tizzy's determination they turned to Jean.

'Listen, we can explain all this if you ask her' (pointing at Tizzy) 'to go away.'

'Why must she go? If you want to talk, you do so in her presence. How do I trust you after what you have just done to me? *She* saved me from vicious *white women*.'

At that point Jean broke down and wept bitterly. Tizzy walked to her bed, sat close to her and comforted her. She took out a crumpled tissue from her dressing gown and gave it to Jean. The latter took it as she continued to sob on Tizzy's shoulder. The women stood there mesmerised by what they saw, but none of them ventured to come near the two girls.

On the following day whispers were afloat about the previous night's happenings. The organisers of the conference decided to defuse the situation by altering the programme. Instead of the usual lunch in the dining hall they suggested that lunchtime be used to deal with issues that were not covered by the programme. Lunch packages were prepared by the caterers for an open session which would allow participants to raise anything they felt strongly about. To give as many people a chance as possible, each speaker was given three minutes only. There was a time keeper and a little bell to monitor the proceedings.

Among those who had something to say was Jean Finney, who very gingerly took the microphone. 'I would like this conference to know that last night I was attacked by a group of white women as I slept in my bed.'

'What's that?'

'Who are those women, for God's sake.'

'How barbaric!'

'Why? Why would they do such a thing?'

These and similar questions were thrown around among the audience. Jean allowed time for this before she continued.

'I need to tell you that this beating had been planned for somebody else, and that is a black woman in this conference. For the past two and half days this conference has been very strong on the need for South African women, black and white, to build a strong spirit of sisterhood across all the existing barriers that bedevil our lives. Secretly a group of white women plotted to do just the opposite. Where is our sincerity if we can't even try to translate our words into actions within the security of a conference like this? What then are we likely to do when we leave here? Where is the sisterhood we are speaking about?'

The reactions grew even wilder at that point.

'Ask the group!'

'Let them come up front to explain themselves!'

The mayoress realised that the situation was getting out of hand. She was worried about what could happen if the group made themselves known to everybody. At that point she intervened. 'Ladies, I would like to say something and I am afraid it will go beyond the three minutes.' Smiling, she half turned to register the remark with the time keeper.

'What we have just heard is very serious. I do not believe it will serve any purpose to stage a court scene. I want to call on the members of 'the group' to meet with the steering committee in the board room this afternoon. This incident tarnishes all of us here and I believe we should make a public apology first to the two young people, secondly to this august conference and thirdly to the notion of sisterhood.

'Before I can even sit down I would like on behalf of this conference to apologise to the two ladies for this unfortunate incident.' By the time she finished, her usual smile had completely disappeared and the heavy tread to her seat confirmed that she was angry. She received a standing ovation for the firm stand she had taken.

'Jean, why didn't you tell me you were going to do this?' asked Tizzy completely overwhelmed by her friend's loyalty and love for her. She had hardly recovered from what Jean had put herself through for her sake on the previous night. Jean did not respond, she simply turned and hugged her. For the first time Tizzy broke down and wept while her friend just clung to her. After a while she pulled out of her arms and turned her tear-drenched face up to Jean; 'I love you Jean. Thanks a ton.'

'Anytime Tiz. That's what sisterhood is about.'

When Tizzy and Jean finished at university they both felt a little pain. They were aware that it would no longer be possible for them to spend as much time together as they had done as room-mates. They took heart in their determination to spend their free time together, and looked forward to the weekends.

Jean secured a job with one of the multinational firms as personnel manager. That company had a substantial number of black workers, both at middle and lower levels. The advert for the job had stressed 'a good understanding and working relationship with blacks'. When she had discussed it with Tizzy, they had both agreed that she was carved out for the job.

At the interview Jean experienced no problem whatsoever; management was overjoyed with her. What impressed them most was the statement Tizzy had prepared on their relationship. In fact one of the interviewers asked Miss Finney if he could contact Miss Khumalo just for interest's sake. To this Jean gladly agreed. What the gentleman got from Tizzy over the phone not only confirmed the contents of her statement, but went further.

Tizzy found a job with the Child Welfare Society in the city. Although the offices were right in the centre of town her responsibility was among black children only. This bothered her a great deal. At the university she had taken the same courses as other students. Social work was social work for her without any colour connotations. The Society was a Child Welfare one without any epithet.

'Why can't we work together for the welfare and well-being of all the children?' she constantly asked herself. What hurt her most was a quiet implication that black children were a lower species of children. That she picked up each time she submitted her reports. There were always negative, derogatory remarks about black children. They were either too many, dirty, undisciplined, little *tsotsis* or some form of delinquent.

'Tizzy, what are you going to do with these little urchins that roam the streets of Hillbrow and Fordsburgh? You have a hell of a job, I am afraid,' her supervisor would always say.

In the office, her white women colleagues marginalised her. She did not feel part of the team at all. She began to question a lot of things whites did in the name of helping blacks. At such moments her friendship with Jean came under review, but at all times one thing was confirmed in her and that was that 'Jean could never be like them.'

These feelings worried Tizzy daily but what she found most frustrating was that she felt utterly helpless in the situation. She had no muscle to change things.

In a very short time Jean bought a house in Rosebank. She phoned Tizzy to tell her the news. They were both excited about it, just like they used to be at Barnato Hall. However, Tizzy's joy had a tinge of sad feelings. At the time she was financially in no position to rent a house in Soweto, let alone buy one. Somehow she managed to dispel her sadness by focusing her thoughts on the fact that she would no longer need to go to Jean's home to see her. Jean's mother was bad news for her. Before they dropped the phones they agreed that they should spend the subsequent weekend together so as to be able to plan for the house-warming party.

At the party Jean introduced Tizzy to Bruce Smithers, her boyfriend. He was a tall and lanky young man who had a slight stoop because of his height. He worked for Barclays Bank, and had done so for five years already. Tizzy noticed something strange when they were introduced. Bruce had a snack in one hand and a glass of wine in the other. When they met he did nothing to put either of these things down so that they could shake hands. He mumbled something and then he was off without the usual niceties. After a little while she dismissed it all telling herself not to ruin the evening. It was truly a lovely party and she met quite a number of the old friends from her student days.

A week later Tizzy dropped in at Jean's place just because she felt at a loose end. She had her own key into the house, and a room too. When she got in she found Jean at dinner with Bruce. Gaily she barged into the kitchen where they were sitting. When Bruce saw Tizzy he clearly showed his displeasure. While the girls were chatting, he unceremoniously left the table. They were both equally surprised.

'Jean, perhaps he doesn't like me,' Tizzy said quickly.

'Rubbish, that's no excuse for rudeness, and to a lady for that matter,' replied Jean, agitated by her boyfriend's behaviour.

She stormed out to find him. He was in the living room sulking behind a newspaper. 'Bruce, what's wrong with you?'

'I should be asking you. I thought you were big enough not to need a nanny any more. She even has her own key into the house. Hm. Imagine. Anyway don't you ever discipline them?'

The kitchen incident brought back the party one in Tizzy's mind. She was no longer in doubt about Bruce's feelings toward her. She quietly tiptoed out through the kitchen door and left the house. The heated dialogue between Jean and Bruce took quite some time so that by the time Jean went back to the kitchen, Tizzy had long gone. She went to her room, but Tizzy was nowhere to be found.

In the end Jean resolved to phone Tizzy first thing on Monday morning, but she was unable to get Tizzy on the phone for the whole of that day in spite of the several messages she left asking her to return her calls. The situation grew from bad to worse.

Matters came to a head when the organisation Tizzy was working for mounted a fund-raising event to which they invited a number of companies they hoped would contribute. The drive was to help initiate a programme for black children. For the first time Tizzy was asked to prepare a paper because it was for the blacks. Suddenly, she became someone who mattered in the organisation.

'Could someone give us a brief rundown of the target figure you're gunning for and how it will be broken down for the different projects?' asked one of the would-be donors.

Very quickly the senior supervisor, Mrs Holloway, called Tizzy aside. From a file under her arm she pulled out a document, explaining hurriedly. 'Look Tizzy dear, Mr Craig would like to know more about *our* plans; what our target is and how we plan to use the money and so on. We believe you are the best person to speak to him.'

Tizzy stood there staring at Mrs Holloway. She was fuming at this blatant attempt at window dressing. She refused to take the file. 'Wait a minute, what are you trying to do to me? When did I ever know there is a target we are working towards? Who drew up this budget?'

'Tizzy, please don't be difficult now, the man is waiting out there. You know as well as I do that these days industry will do anything in the name of community involvement. You know that.'

At that point Mrs Holloway pushed the file under Tizzy's arm, who raised her elbow and let the file drop right where they stood, bracing herself for Mrs Holloway's next move.

'There has been no time to explain things in detail to you, I admit,' apologised Mrs Holloway. 'Everyone is so busy trying to find money for the whole organisation since the rand dropped. This is our big chance.'

'So *I* must be a ladder to use. And *my* people the bait at the end of the hook?'

Mrs Holloway could no longer hide the fact that she was utterly fed-up with Tizzy.

'Tizzy what on earth do you think you are doing?' she lashed out. 'Have you forgotten who your supervisor is in this association? Do I have to remind you on such an important occasion?'

'Do I have to make a fool of myself in order to prove to you I know who my supervisor is? Since when am I expected to do my boss's work? You tell me?' quizzed Tizzy, equally fuming.

'This is gross insubordination. Do you know that this

81

behaviour of yours can cost you dearly?'

'Go ahead Mrs Holloway; who cares!' and Tizzy stormed out of the office.

As she stood at the entrance she recognised a very executive-looking young woman in earnest conversation with two gentlemen in dark suits. For a moment she stood there trying to make sure she wasn't mistaken. The Bruce incident flashed back for a brief moment. Just then the threesome broke into a loud laughter.

'Yes, that *is* Jean, I just couldn't be wrong, I knew it,' remarked Tizzy to herself. She began to move slowly towards them. Jean had her back towards her so that it was one of the two men who made her aware of Tizzy's approach. She swung round to meet Tizzy's eyes and there was a silence.

'Hi Jean!'

To her shock and utter disgust Jean did not even smile. 'Good morning, can I help you?'

Tizzy did not believe she had heard her right. For some time she couldn't see, although here eyes were wide open. Then she decided to start again. 'Jean Finney?'

One of the gentlemen quickly interjected, 'Excuse me, do you know Miss Finney?'

She deliberately did not respond to the question. Flashbacks of her encounter with Mrs Holloway flooded her mind. She also remembered for the first time that when Jean had applied for her present prestigious job, the fact that she had had such a close relationship with a black woman for that length of time had been her strongest recommendation. And this was what had become of her!

She felt she had indeed been used. Even, looking back, that Jean had used her to gain acceptance on the campus across the colour line. She had always joined the black students when they were out there demonstrating against the Quota System. She had made her believe they were South Africans together. Damn it, she had used her to procure her present job which made her personnel officer for the blacks in the company. How could she do this to her? The questions kept resounding in her ears.

At 'varsity, they had both been critical of black people being subjected to academic research.

'What's the point of all this research which only helps a few to acquire PhDs and Masters while people still stay poor?' Jean used to argue. This Tizzy recalled so clearly. It was at a faculty meeting where they were being encouraged to undertake research.

She herself had stood up to say, 'My biggest worry is that these researchers, who are predominantly white, only manage to gain recognition for themselves both locally and internationally on our suffering.'

When she sat down there had been a hefty round of applause, particularly from the corner which had a concentration of black students. One of them had shouted, 'If it's a big name you want, or a quick buck, invade the black situation – that's a commercial.' A guffaw of laughter had followed which took quite some time to die down.

When she eventually snapped out of her reverie, Jean and her colleagues had already moved away. She did not even want to find out where they had gone.

Six months later the managing director of Jean's company called a senior staff meeting. Although Jean was not a senior, she was invited to attend because of her background, particularly her strong links with and understanding of blacks. The director passed round photographs of three vehicles that had been burnt out in Soweto.

'Ladies and gentlemen I do not need to tell you what those photos mean in terms of money that went up in flames, so to speak. The big question that faces us now is what can we do as a company?'

'These good-for-nothing urchins need to be taught a lesson by someone,' said Mr Forbes, the deputy managing director.

'But what on earth is it that these children want? They burn the schools (*their* schools, mind you), they burn delivery vehicles and the deliveries are for *their* good, not for ours?' asked Mr Thompson the sales manager, visibly agitated.

The director decided to intervene. 'Ladies and Gentlemen, let's not delude ourselves. We all know the answer to those questions, each one of them. What do they want? They know what they want and they have told us in no uncertain terms. So I repeat, let's not delude ourselves. Too much is at stake. Let's be practical and talk about where we go from here.'

'Action is what we need and in terms of the demands that have been made. Miss Finney, that's your turf. You should guide us.' Mr Forbes challenged Jean.

'OK I think I can work on this but I need a bit of time to put it all together.'

Tizzy was in the office when the call from Jean came in.

'Good morning, Jean Finney here. Can I speak to Tizzy Khumalo?'

Tizzy did a double take on that one. 'I beg your pardon, the line is very bad this side, come again.'

'My name is Jean Finney and I would like to speak to Tizzy, if I may.'

Tizzy was no longer in doubt. It was Jean. She swallowed some air, dropped her voice, and responded. 'Speaking, can I help you?'

'Oh, I am so glad I caught you in the office, I expect you are extremely busy with all that is going on in the townships.' Jean was genuinely delighted to get through to Tizzy, particularly because of the problem on her hands. This challenge meant a lot to her and her future in the company. To deal with it successfully she knew very well that she needed Tizzy desperately, and she was prepared to bend over backwards, if need be, to get it. She had not forgotten how they had parted but she half hoped that enough water would have flowed under the bridge for them to get together again.

When Tizzy heard Jean's voice on the phone she remembered the Mrs Holloway scene, the scene in the hall, and in particular Jean's cold executive face that morning. She remembered the statement she had made about Jean the day she had gone for her interview. Again she felt her friend had successfully used her, but what incensed her most was the sneaking feeling that Jean wanted to use her again.

'Could you come to the point please, I don't have an eternity before me, Jean.'

'I thought we could have lunch together one of these days for old times' sake. How does that strike you? We have a lot to catch up on, don't we?'

To Tizzy 'old times' sake' spelt all the instances Jean had used her for her own gain. 'Actually I am struggling very hard to erase "old times" with you from my memory, Miss Finney. If what you did to me calls for a celebration for you, I am sorry that's not where I am at, Miss Finney. I have nothing to celebrate.'

'Tizzy, perhaps I need to come out straight, my company is gravely concerned about what is going on in the townships and they wish to help as much as they can. So I thought I could pick your brains.'

'Is there a promotion in the offing?'

'What do you mean? I don't understand. Look let's not quiz each other when some child might be dying in one of the townships right this very moment. I'm prepared to come to your office for a discussion if that suits you.'

'Jean every right-thinking black is just fed-up with you liberals. Any time you want something it's a black you must use. But when you don't need us you can't be bothered.'

'I'm surprised at your anger, Tizzy, I was just trying to be helpful. This situation touches all of us. You can't deny that.'

'Indeed, it does, but in different ways. Some are concerned about their careers, while for others it's our homes that are going up in flames. So my question still stands unanswered – is there a promotion in the offing?'

'Why do you connect this with a promotion, Tizzy?'

'You whites do it so often you don't even see yourselves any more. Look back at our supposed good days together and get beneath that relationship. What the purpose was; for whose benefit? It led straight up to your present job?'

'Tizzy in any relationship, good relationship, there are gains on both sides. They may not be 50/50 but they are definitely there, you can't deny that at least.'

'I used to think like that Jean, but on reflection I have found out I was a fool to let you use me all that time. Now I know better and no white is ever going to use me again. I would rather be used by other blacks. They can never set me up and get me kicked out of their houses, ever.'

'Has all this something to do with Bruce? Now I see. Tizzy, I have tried my damndest to get to you so that I could explain things, but to no avail. Now I'm no longer sure you were not avoiding me all this time.'

'What does it matter, Jean? You are white and I am black. That's what matters in this country and it looks like life can never be lived on a human level in this land.'

Women and the law

DEATH OF A MISSIONARY

Elsa Joubert

The missionary's wife went out to the garden in the early morning. As she walked down the path her hands almost unconsciously reached out to touch the flowers and to feel the moist dew on the leaves. Her fingers lingered when she came to the roses, trembling as she touched the rosebuds.

At the gate she heard the milkman coming round the corner. 'My husband passed away last night.'

The milkman had often found the missionary in the rose garden in the early mornings. He took off his hat. 'Oh, missus!'

'But he wasn't in pain – he went peacefully,' said the missionary's wife. 'He wasn't young any more. His time had come.' The milkman stood silently with her for a few moments, then she heard the clink of his milk basket going down the street again.

The nurse was still in the house. Her sister, who'd come to support her through the last days, was on the verandah.

'I've got coffee ready in the kitchen. Come and have a cup.'

'Did you take some to the nurse?'

'Yes. She has everything she needs.'

When she'd drunk her coffee, she said, 'There's a hat in the box on the cupboard in the spare room. And a jacket in the wardrobe. Please bring them for me. It seems to have turned rather chilly.'

Her sister fetched the things and she put them on in the bathroom.

Her sister turned her face, so that she looked into her eyes. 'Mary, surely you don't mean to go out?'

'Oh, is it too early?' asked the missionary's wife. 'Is it too early to go? Surely it's gone eight?'

'It is after eight. Where are you off to?'

'To the minister. Before he goes out. I must discuss the funeral with him. The sooner the better.'

'But won't the undertakers. . . .'

The missionary's wife shook her head. 'I want to speak to the minister.'

When she reached the pavement she felt unsteady on her legs and it surprised her because she had faced the fact of her husband's passing for so long. She had lived with it. She made a determined effort to put the face in the sickroom out of her mind for a while, just to give her strength for what lay ahead; and, thanks to long years of practising self-control, she succeeded. Her step became firmer.

She didn't come across anyone she knew because it was so early. Except the washerwoman with her baby tied on to her back. In the same tone she'd used for the milkman, she said, 'My husband died last night.'

The washerwoman took both her hands and squeezed them. 'Oh, my missus!'

She could still feel the warmth of the woman's hands as she walked on.

When she pushed open the minister's gate, the children rushed out, on their way to school. The front door was still open and it wasn't necessary to ring the bell because the housemaid was polishing the passage floor.

'Would old missus like to see the madam?'

'No, I want to talk to the minister.'

For the first time, as she sat in the straight-backed chair in the study, waiting for the minister, her emotions threatened to get the better of her. Her lower lip began to tremble and her throat closed. Her hands shook so she had to clasp them together in her lap. She was glad she was wearing the jacket.

She was very fond of the young minister. He put his arm around her shoulders.

'My dear friend?' There was something like dread mingled with the compassion in his question.

The tears welled up as she nodded and dabbed her eyes with her handkerchief.

He'd known of the missionary's illness and that the end couldn't be far.

88

'Last night?'

She nodded again.

'And were you alone?' He was really saying: why didn't you send for me? But then he realised: how could she, in the night, when she was alone?

'My sister has been with me for the last few days. But she couldn't come for you on her own, after dark.'

The missionary's wife tucked her handkerchief into her bag because the weakness had passed for the time being.

'His is not the first passing I've witnessed. The doctor came early this morning and he sent for the nurse.'

The young minister bowed his head. 'The reverend didn't need me, he was ready to meet his Maker. If there was ever anyone who was prepared. . . .' He took her cold hands in his. 'We will miss him.'

She didn't answer.

'Everyone loved him. One of the chosen few. . . .'

His words began to undermine her self-control. Her tone became more matter of fact.

'I came to discuss his funeral. I would like you to conduct the service.'

It clearly amazed him that she had come to arrange this so soon after his death, so early, alone – without the support of family or friends.

'It would be a privilege,' he answered. He called to his wife, 'Can we have a tray of tea, please. And, Christine, will you come here a minute?'

His wife was young. She was still busy with her chores so she hadn't changed from her housecoat. She held it closed in front, apologetically. 'I had to get the children off, you know.'

Her husband cut her short. 'Her husband died last night. She has come to talk to me about the funeral.'

The young woman had never met him, but she'd known about the minister who lay ill for so long in one of the streets on the other side of town. She felt guilty as she pressed her cheek briefly against the older woman's. 'My deepest sympathy, my dear.' They were acquainted through various women's organizations. 'Death will have its way. And he was ill for so long.' She stumbled over the words. 'I'll make tea.'

The missionary's wife sat down again. 'We can arrange the

funeral for the day after tomorrow,' she said, 'if my brothers, especially the one furthest away, are to come. Though none of them is young any more, so I don't know. . . . But I particularly want his old congregation to have the chance to come – from Ebenhaezer. You know, my husband preached in that mission church for thirty years. They loved him.'

The young minister had gone to his desk to write down the date and time. 'Three in the afternoon?'

'That would do.'

'I would like you,' said the missionary wife, 'to allocate enough space in the church for his parish council and the retired council members who served under him. The young preacher – one of their own people – will also come. My husband offered his life to the people of Ebenhaezer. We built the church, thanks be to God.' The ghost of a smile played across her pale face. 'It will mean a lot to me to see them again.'

'You say a number of your husband's old congregation will come?' asked the young minister.

'I think so. A funeral is important. One can hire buses. And it isn't that far. A three- or four-hour journey.'

The young minister jotted down some notes with his pencil. 'I would imagine about half the church?'

There was not a large church in this town where they'd retired to live in peace and quiet, still devoted to the service of the Lord.

She nodded.

'I won't stay for tea. Please thank your wife for me. I'd better be going.'

'Can I accompany you?'

'I'll be fine. It isn't far.'

But he saw her to the gate and lingered there, his eyes following her.

Her footsteps were brisker than they'd been when she walked down the garden path with him. It was as though something was driving her home – or rather drawing her. The old minister. Such love and devotion was truly moving. And her acceptance of God's will made him feel humble.

During the course of the morning, the undertakers removed the earthly remains of the Lord's old servant and then the house was empty.

It remained empty even though friends and neighbours –

people who'd grown attached to them over the last five years – came by to offer their condolences. The missionary's wife sat on the front verandah as dusk fell. The scent of roses was a comfort to her as she rested in the chair with its faded cushion. It was a wicker rocking chair, one of a pair made by a blind member of her husband's old congregation. She loved this chair. Her husband used to sit in the opposite one of an evening, at this time when the fragrance of the roses was so sweet – especially when the garden was damp.

She sat so still that the minister didn't like to disturb her.

He thought she hadn't seen him draw nearer in the half light, but she said, 'Please sit down. It was good of you to come. Sit there. It was my husband's chair.'

The minister was not happy. She could feel his discomfort and while this morning it had been he who put a consoling arm around her shoulders, it was she who now felt: I must comfort him.

'What is troubling you?' she asked gently.

The words were heavy. He fiddled with the wicker of the chair, and the familiar movement sent a surprising shaft of pain through her heart.

Then he spoke. 'As a servant of the Lord it is very difficult for me to say what I have to. But I have no choice.'

She couldn't imagine what he could possibly be talking about. All they had discussed up to now was the funeral.

'The funeral?' she prompted.

He spoke quickly. 'I was obliged to consult members of the church council, and they instructed me to call a full council meeting this afternoon. It will not be possible to set aside seating for the members of your husband's old congregation.'

In his embarrassment, he spoke more brusquely than he'd meant to. If it had only been up to him. . . . He had tried to sway the council, tried to guide their reasoning, but in vain. So many coloureds . . . they'd refused.

His last words were hopeless. 'They simply won't compromise.'

'I understand,' said the missionary's wife. 'I'm sorry.' Her words were proper. If he hadn't already arisen from her husband's chair, she would have reached out a hand to touch his, to soften the message he brought.

'I am sorry I have put you in this awkward position.'

'I'm not in an awkward position.'

Her manner made him colour. If only she'd been sad, angry or, at least, put out!

'But what will you do? Will you compromise? I hate to think what you are going to tell his old congregation. We don't want to hurt any feelings.'

A church bell began to toll far away in the lower town. It sounded the answer to the question that hung in the air between them. Her husband had often told her: *If you don't know the answer, ask the Lord. Have faith. He won't keep you waiting.* A smile, painful in its sweetness, visible even in the failing light, warmed her face. It seemed as though she was in touch with her husband or with God, or both.

'We don't hurt any feelings.'

The bell tolled in the mission church across the river where the houses were poorer, the gardens smaller. The washerwoman, and the milk delivery man had both come from there that morning.

'We know the minister at the mission,' said the late missionary's wife. 'He and my husband often prayed together in the little church where that bell is ringing now. My husband was always so pleased if one of their own people could take office for them. I will go there. They can bury him from there. That way we won't offend anyone.'

She allowed the minister to give them a lift to the river – this time her sister insisted on coming too. The missionary's wife made him drop them at the bridge.

'I don't mind walking, minister,' she assured him. 'Neither does my sister. We'd rather go on alone. They'll send a youngster back with us.'

He turned the car in the dirt road and they got out.

They walked slowly, feeling the strain as they went up the rise on the other side of the river, careful not to step in a wet or fouled spot – animals still roamed free around here. It was already quite dark.

'Here's the cottage,' said the missionary's wife.

They pushed the small gate open and walked up the path to the verandah steps.

Then they paused. The wood-and-iron house was white-washed like the church.

The sister linked one hand through Mary's arm and used the other to grasp the railing for support. The iron was cold under her hand. She felt miserable.

'I can manage,' said the missionary's wife, her tread steadier than her sister's.

The minister's face first lit up and then darkened when he saw who it was knocking at his door.

'Please come in!' He stood back to draw them in. His stocky figure seemed to fill the whole passage. He had just got up from the table. He had part of his black suit on – he was still in his shirt-sleeves and his serviette was thrust in under the second button of his waistcoat.

He'd forgotten to remove the serviette. He offered the two women chairs that were too deep – plush chairs bought second-hand in the upper town. They sank uncomfortably into them.

'I'm pleased you're here!' With difficulty (because he wasn't built for it) the minister sank to his knees before the missionary's wife.

Uncertainly, he started to reach his hands out to her. She rose from her chair and put her hand in his. His brown hands covered her old white one.

'I heard of the reverend's death. I was planning to come today, but I thought: let me give your own people a chance to comfort you today and I'll come tomorrow.'

'You should have come today,' said the woman softly while he held her hand. 'You loved him.'

Tears streamed down the brown minister's face. He wasn't aware of them until he felt the moisture drip, then he wiped his eyes with the serviette still hanging from his waistcoat.

'He was a father to me. More than a father. In the hard task. . . .'

'He loved you too.'

She heard the clink of crockery in the kitchen. She remembered the service he would have to attend shortly. Had he finished eating?

He got up off his knees and turned to her sister. 'Excuse me, I should have . . . I would like to extend my sympathy to you as well.'

93

Then he sat down, legs splayed, fingers together, looking at them questioningly. There must be some reason why they were here tonight.

'I would like you to bury him, reverend,' said the missionary's wife.

He didn't understand at first. 'Say a few words at the graveside?'

Again the shadow of a smile puckered her mouth. 'No, reverend, bury him.' She pointed to the side of the house where the church stood. 'From here. From the missionary church.'

He threw up his hands. 'Was that his wish? He didn't know many of us over on this side of the river. He always said: "It's your flock, retired people mustn't meddle with another man's congregation." Not many people here knew him.'

The missionary's wife couldn't pretend. 'No, I can't say it was his wish, but it is my wish. A few busloads of people from his old congregation at Ebenhaezer will come to the funeral. That's why I am here tonight, I must let them know tomorrow.'

Her voice was weary. Her face looked drained in the dull gold light of the lamp, as though she too had died. Her sister stood up. 'Come on Mary, we must get back. You need some rest.' She explained to the reverend: 'She didn't sleep a wink last night. She's exhausted.'

They helped her up out of the chair. The reverend said: 'It would be a great honour to conduct the funeral service here in my church – the church where we prayed together. Perhaps this is the way it was meant to be.' He would see to the arrangements for the hearse and the graveyard later.

But she had one more thing to sort out. Remembering her promise to the minister, she said: 'His friends from Ebenhaezer aren't the only consideration.'

Before he'd given up and driven them to the river, the minister had tried to dissuade them, stressing that: 'We were also his friends. We of the upper town.' He mentioned names – their neighbours, the church council, members of the women's organization and their husbands, farmers in the district. 'We also want to be there. We want a block for at least fifty people. You must insist on that.'

'Could you reserve a place in the church for say thirty or forty of his other people?' She gestured wearily towards the other side of the river. 'For our friends over there. . . .'

The reverend nodded. 'Of course.'

His visible sorrow brought hers up from the depths where she had buried it. Lines of pain crumpled her face. She clung to his hand. Her sister started to weep. She forgave her brother-in-law that the two of them – two women alone – had to be here now, at night, in this situation.

'He was a good man,' she said. 'So kind and tolerant.'

The missionary's wife was the first to regain her composure. 'You must be going.' She knew it was time for his service.

'I can't allow you to leave like this.' He called down the passage for a child who came forward inquisitively but shyly. He took the child by the shoulder. 'Run down the road to your uncle. Tell him he must bring his taxi right away. Off you go.'

'Won't you sit down again? I have to go but the taxi will be here in a minute. I'm sorry I can't stay. My wife will bring you some tea.'

'Don't worry about the tea,' said the sister. 'I must get her home. I'm tremendously relieved about the taxi.'

Nearby they could already hear the congregation singing. The ineffable sweetness of the allelujahs was like a balm. The missionary's wife was almost sorry when the child announced that the car had arrived, and she and her sister felt their way down the steps and climbed through the large old-fashioned door the driver held open for them. But they were grateful not to have to walk home. The little boy who'd summoned the car jumped into the front passenger seat. They bumped along the dirt track and then turned into the road that led across the bridge to the upper town.

Over the bridge they saw the tail-lights of a car drawn on to the dirt road where the minister had dropped them earlier.

The child, who studied cars, and particularly this one, forgot his shyness and said, 'It's the minister's car.'

'Oh my, that means he waited,' said the sister.

'Or came back to fetch us,' said the missionary's wife.

But it was too late to stop, they'd overshot it by too much. 'If he's still there when you come back, please tell him we've gone,' she asked the driver.

He wouldn't allow them to pay. 'Let's just say it was for the old reverend,' he said as he held the door open for them and then unclipped the garden gate. 'I heard about your loss. Everything is different when someone dies. 'Specially when it's him.'

She must have slept that night because when she heard her sister Ella busy with the cups early next morning, she didn't recall having lain awake.

The Lord is good to me, she thought. *He prepared me for a long time and He won't deny me the gift of acceptance now.*

She looked tenderly at his bed. It was covered with a counterpane, but she wanted to make it up properly again.

She was dressed and pinning her hair up before the mirror when she heard the garden gate open. Through the lace curtains, she could see the brown minister walking up the path. He knocked at the front door and hesitated on the threshold until she insisted he come in. 'Please sit down.' She couldn't remember his visiting her husband. Did they ever pray together here? she wondered vaguely . . . but she couldn't get a grip on her thoughts this morning.

'No, in here,' she said. 'Please sit down.'

The morning breeze was still chilly outside so she closed the front door.

The house was small and the hallway doubled as a sitting room.

He wore his black jacket and a white shirt. He held his hat and sat uncomfortably on the straight-backed chair which had seemed to be the nearest to him.

'It is hard for me to say this to you. Your husband was a good man. He was one of the Lord's chosen ones. We loved him. I want to bury him from my church. It will be a blessing on our church to carry him out from there.'

'What is the problem then, reverend?' the missionary's wife asked.

'There was some trouble last night after the service. Someone spread the story that the other church would not reserve a block for his old congregation. They are upset about this. They say in that case he is ours. We are not going to set aside a block for them.'

The brown minister was so distressed that tears sprang to his eyes. 'He was a father to me. I want to open my church. I want to say: "Let everyone who loved him come." But the church council won't permit it.'

He even forgot the embarrassment of sitting in a white woman's sitting room, or the embarrassment of her sister. His grief for his betrayed friend ran very deep, but from somewhere, somewhere else, may God forgive him, came the thought: *It's only fair. That'll teach them.* Thus spoke the serpent in his bosom, the devil that stalked him. If possible, his self-disgust was more intense than his sadness. He tried to suppress it.

'I tried.' Once again he held his hands up to her. 'I tried. But they wouldn't agree. They said: family and relatives, yes, but not them – not the poeple from the upper church who refused us.'

'The minister?'

'They said no, not the minister. . . .'

She thought of the soft clear face of the young minister who'd been with her yesterday, of the friends who'd come during the night, bringing their offerings of cakes and puddings and flowers – trifles, but nonetheless symbols of love.

'We can't hurt them,' she said quietly to the brown minister before her.

He stood up. 'I'll bring the subject up again,' he said, but he knew it was hopeless.

'What now?' asked her sister when she'd gone. 'I knew this love-thy-brother attitude of yours. . . . If you set yourself up as too holy, God punishes you. Now you'll have to bury him in the veld.' Ashamed, she checked herself. 'Can we take him back to his old parish?' she asked quietly with real compassion.

The missionary's wife shook her head. 'He can't lie buried out there so far from home.' The weariness, which she could only temporarily shake off, crept up on her – starting from the soles of her feet and moving slowly up through her body until she was as white as a sheet, and had to sit down again. 'It's so far. We'd have to bring him back here after the service, and then would they allow us to lay him to rest in our graveyard? After all the bad feelings? Would he *want* to be buried there?'

Oh, Lord, she prayed, *Could You not bear him up like Elijah? What must I do with the scraps of bone and tired flesh that remain of my husband?*

Lord, in your infinite mercy, could You not prevent his body from becoming a hindrance to your children? Is he to be a stumbling block in death where in life he was not? Can You not send down Your fire to consume him? His spirit served You. Are his mortal remains to stand in the way of Your all-wise clemency?

And now for the first time, her tears flowed freely. But if his work is not yet done, Lord, if his body is to be an instrument of wrath in Your hands, let it be according to Your will.

HUNGRY IN A RICH LAND

Ellen Kuzwayo

Love of adventure and a desire to explore the unknown seem to be the two forces which motivated about 1 to 5 per cent of the early black voluntary migrant labourers to leave their rural homes for the first industrial settlements. This was at the close of the nineteenth century, when gold and diamonds were discovered in South Africa. The rapid growth of these industries demanded more and more workers, and this demand could not be met by the gradual flow of migrant labourers trickling into the new cities.

That black people at that time were owners of the land they tilled and cultivated; that they formed a community with an established culture and moral code as well as a valid economic structure; these factors, together with many others which contributed to the stability and prosperity of individual families, meant that the majority of the black population found no pressing need to leave their homes to go in search of employment.

It was very unfotunate that the early colonists of this country developed some of the most inhuman and destabilising administrative laws to control the movement and lives of black people in an effort to push them out of their homes and pull them into the new industrial places for the benefit of those industries and to the detriment of the total black society. Is it surprising that this country is now paying heavily for these injustices?

The following are but a few of the laws formulated to promote, regulate and enforce the migrant labour system:

- The 1913 Land Act which disinherited black people from their right to own land in freehold.
- The culling of livestock. Up to that time blacks were

successful livestock farmers. Now regulations controlled the size of their herds.

- The implementation of a poll tax levied on every black man. He was compelled to pay this in cash. He was forbidden in some way to sell stock or grain to raise the amount.

These laws were introduced to push black men out of their homes: fathers, husbands and sons. They were not even compensated by being paid a living wage with which they could support the families they left behind.

As industry grew, more stringent and complex legislation was brought in which did not take into the account the skills which black workers had acquired in the various industries. Job reservation laws were passed to debar blacks from doing certain jobs, thereby protecting white workers against any possible competition from black workers.

Influx control regulations secured the migrant labour system. This was legislation that made it impossible for families to live with or visit their men where they worked – even for a week. Such visitors, if permitted to come to the cities, were given only 72 hours to be there.

It is frightening to imagine life in the compounds where men are locked up for at least nine months, on contract, without a visit from their wives. Similarly those wives are left behind for all that time. The alarming question is – what remains of family life at their reunion? Materialism is rated far above human values by the people who make such laws.

Influx control laws have been used systematically to entrench the migrant labour system, to dispossess black people of their citizenship, their private and communal land, and finally to throw them into some desolate undeveloped parts of South Africa – called 'homelands' – all reservoirs of cheap migrant labour for wealthy South Africa. People are forced into these undeveloped areas, where there are no jobs, no health service, no schools.

As most responsible black leaders with credibility among the people refuse to serve as puppets of the government, the white powers have been compelled to appoint persons who are willing to carry out their policies at the expense of those they are supposed to represent! In addition, these officials are not provided with enough revenue, or even training, which would enable them to run the institutions in an acceptable manner.

It is against this background that we should explore the lives of those who are left behind without fathers, husbands, or sons. These are women; mothers, wives, thousands of them, left to fend for themselves and those in their care – children and old people. It will be revealing to assess the effect migrant labour has had on their lives, and on their families and communities.

Let me share with you the case history of a community I worked with for twelve years, from 1964 to 1975, when, as a social worker, I was General Secretary of the Young Women's Christian Association in the Transvaal.

The area of my work stretched from the Vaal River in the south, included Johannesburg and the rest of the Witwatersrand – as well as Pretoria – and was bounded in the north by the Louis Trichardt district. This particular case history study was in the Zoutpansberg area. Here the evils, the harsh cruelties and inhumanities of the migrant labour system, were revealed to me.

I had started my work in urban communities where families, by and large, were a complete unit, with a mother, a father, and children. This gave me a false picture of what to expect in rural areas, where I soon found that more than three-quarters of the families were without husbands and fathers. They were away from home, gone on migrant labour contracts to one industrial area or another. This was a shocking revelation to me.

It was September 1964. My journey took me nearly 200 miles from Johannesburg. The moment I stepped off the train at Louis Trichardt, I saw a vast difference in the surrounding countryside, which had vivid scars of the severe drought which had been raging in that area for three successive years. The effect of the drought was hanging on every face on that station. Each person seemed to carry a heavy burden on their shoulders; their feet and knees and whole body sagged as if under some invisible load. I was struck by what seemed to be an infectious, depressing atmosphere.

As it was my first visit to that area, I was preoccupied with my arrival at my destination; how was I going to get there, and who would take me? I was relieved when a gentleman enquired who I was. Still struck by what I was seeing around me, I was grateful

101

to move away from that scene. We travelled through a very dry, barren countryside, and in intense heat.

On my arrival in Valdezia, a Swiss Mission Church settlement, I found women, young mothers, some nursing infants or toddlers. About forty-five of the women came from the traditional neighbouring rural communities established in about a five-mile radius around the mission station. Valdezia was about eight miles away from Elim – the nearest and only hospital in that area.

Another group came from a new resettlement camp, Malamulela, which was sited further north. Here were hundreds of uprooted families who had succumbed to removal. From their appearance and dress, the majority of these women came also from a traditional background.

I was reassured by the warm welcome I received. As I moved around to talk to the women, I noticed that the children with them were not enjoying good health. Some had swollen shining feet, hands, abdomens, puffed faces. They were listless and moaned in an unsettled manner. Although the women were there physically, they were emotionally distant to what was happening. Their uneasiness was apparent and disturbing. Later I was told that there was a gastro-enteritis epidemic in the area, which was affecting them.

The President of the Zoutpansberg area of the YWCA was the wife of the local librarian, an enlightened woman whose family was one of the first to have contact with the missionaries in that area. She welcomed me and, understanding at once the uneasiness I felt at what I was seeing, she told me that many families in the Zoutpansberg were going without food for days. I heard that some of the women had walked eight miles from their homes to attend the event for the sole purpose of getting a meal. She explained that the hunger was caused by the persisting drought, and furthermore, that many husbands, away on migrant labour in the cities and towns, were not coming home or sending money regularly to their families.

The menu for the day was a broth of bones and sinews cooking in a large three-legged pot. There was another pot of *mielie-pap* (corn-meal porridge). The President told me that their club faced financial problems, concluding that the meal was the best they could afford. I was both hurt and embarrassed. I did not have the courage to eat the lunch I had brought for myself. Small as it was, I gave it to her to be served with the rest of the meal. I was ashamed of the clothes I was wearing. It was at that point that the committee decided to change the order of the programme. The meal was hurriedly prepared so that it preceded the discussion because we realised that many women would not participate fully if they were hungry.

The next item after the meal was an assessment of the local situation to enable me to give an authentic report to the Board of Management. It was summed up thus:

- The three years' severe drought had immobilised the women's yearly programme of tilling the land and growing food to supplement the irregular low wages from their husbands away on migrant labour.
- Both the traditional villages surrounding the mission station and the newly resettled community were hard hit by the drought and the serious shortage of water, but the effect of these was more apparent in the resettled community. Black people are by culture and tradition a sharing community, helping each other when food and services are needed. Their generous hospitality, regardless of whether the visitor has been invited or expected, and their community service system, arranged through work camps when major tasks are needed to be done, both these are demonstrations of their communal way of life. Deaths, marriages, celebrations of all kinds are a shared responsibility in the black community.

  The fact that the resettlement was still too recent for the residents to know one another, and that family structures had been broken up, made it impossible for the people to care for each other in the traditional way.
- Prior to this time of want and starvation, when black communities tilled their own land and raised their own livestock, when wild vegetation was a common dish, children's diseases like kwashiorkor and gastro-enteritis, both diseases related to poverty, were unknown. Worse still, mothers were now left to cope on their own. The death of many children made the situation bleak.
- More than three-quarters of the husbands of the women attending the event were away on migrant labour contracts.

Few visited home regularly every month, or sent money home if they failed to come. Many sent money at irregular intervals, and visited once in while. The rest did not send money, or write, or visit. Most husbands in this category had established new families where they worked.

This outline of the problem was revealing, startling and overwhelming. The reality of the devastating effects of the migrant labour system, its implications and extent were brought home to me for the first time. I was shocked more than words can express. The problem seemed too wide and deep to know where to start.

I recognised a desperate, complex situation which needed immediate urgent action. My response was to share my findings with my Board of Management. The YWCA is a voluntary organisation which took upon itself the task of assisting communities hit by government laws. It is an organisation of black women, who are, ironically, still categorised by the state as minors, children. In situations like these, women are heroines.

We know that the effects of migrant labour are seen on different levels. We experience separation from our menfolk, we have to survive on the low wages the men earn, and we have to endure starvation. We must help ourselves because we know that the South African government is unconcerned and without pity for the suffering and struggle of the black people.

One of the objectives of the YWCA is to help communities regain their strength and to give them confidence to help themselves. Their fund-raising and appeals are for these projects.

After hurried but in-depth consultations, the outline of a strategy to deal with the situation was formulated into short- and long-term objectives, as follows:

Short-term objectives

- To identify the best nourishing powdered milk on the market, purchase it and have it delivered to the Zoutpansberg Executive Committee of the YWCA. To emphasise the importance of using the milk with every meal, paticularly for growing children.
- To supply only two kinds of seeds – spinach and tomato – to keen willing members, to stress the need to start very small

patches of vegetable gardens using any dirty water for watering the plants.

- To launch intensive educational programmes on the correct feeding of infants, using local people with expertise – missionaries, nurses, doctors. That these local people had not themselves initiated any such programme must be due in some measure to their preoccupation with the functioning of their own institutions, but also, and more particularly, to their inability to organise the women and mobilise them into a group effort.

Long-term objectives

- To ensure a regular supply of powdered milk, and its regular use.
- To support members cultivating vegetable gardens, and to encourage them to eat raw tomatoes.
- To support those already running infant feeding schemes. They were to be visited monthly or bi-monthly to give practical and emotional support to those involved.
- To motivate women to use skills they already knew, working with beads and wild grasses, or to learn new skills like sewing, knitting and weaving. Women embarked on producing school uniforms, making tunics and knitting school jerseys. They made uniforms for church women's groups. They wove covers for sofas and other household furniture. They were organising themselves into cottage industries.

Mostly they worked to fulfil orders, which eliminated the need to search for a market. Products not made to order were sold locally, at events like a Christmas market, when women had received some money from their husbands, sons or fathers.

Board members also bought some of the products to help the women generate some income. I remember several occasions when I transported school uniforms, jerseys and tunics made by women in the Zoutpansberg to schools in Soweto. I shared with the producers a common feeling of achievement and satisfaction in a task accomplished.

I still felt the situation was too great for one organisation to handle on its own, so I decided to scout for human resources around the Zoutpansberg so that I could form a team which would work out a strategy to alleviate the imminent disaster facing the community. I was encouraged when the missionary's wife agreed to assist us, and together we contacted the doctors at Elim hospital, and the local agricultural demonstrators. This team was reinforced by nurses and teachers who were themselves members of the Zoutpansberg YWCA.

Undermined as it was by such a malady of deprivation and dispossession, the community had over the past three years lost some of its old cultural practices. The surroundings of the villages were no longer clean. The mothers became more and more overwhelmed by the deteriorating condition of their children's health. Cases of kwashiorkor and gastro-enteritis surfaced daily in the community leaving the children debilitated, or causing their death.

The team of professional experts was thus called upon to address this calamity; to restore the old cultural values and customs in the community; to reinforce these where necessary with new health services which the community could undertake. The women's response to the recommendations made by this team had resounding, rewarding results. The most visible was the erection of individual, homestead toilets in the traditional villages. The project was supervised by the agricultural demonstrators, knowledgeable in the laying of pit system toilets.

The women grouped themselves into work-camp units. Each unit decided on who they would include, and on the size of their unit. Each woman provided her own building materials, according to the specifications given by the agricultural demonstrators. When the question of the cost was raised, the women unanimously decided that it was their responsibility and that it be left in their care.

The six-feet deep pits were dug by each work-camp unit on the selected day, and at a specified home. The building and inserting of the toilet seat was organised in the same fashion, under the supervision of the agricultural demonstrators, as was the roofing and the whitewashing of the toilet walls. Of the thirty or more toilets erected, all but one withstood the heavy, stormy summer rains which fell within the first twelve months. This group of women who embarked on building the pit system toilets became an inspiration in that area, and with the change of conditions for the better, more and more women joined the project.

The outcome of all these efforts exceeded all expectations.

Kwashiorkor gradually disappeared with the regular use of powdered milk and scanty vegetables.

Gastro-enteritis responded well to the intensive disposal of faeces through their burial in deep holes, prior to the erection of the toilets which finally brought that killer to a stop.

The unexpectedly positive results from the classes in correct infant feeding run by the missionary's wife became a motivation for the local mothers.

The message of the re-birth of that community spread. It reached some husbands who had 'deserted' their homes because of the burden of the migrant labour system. Some of them returned to visit their homes again. Like in every situation, there were casualties who never responded to the good news.

My visit to the Zoutpansberg three months after those summer rains is still vivid in my mind. I stood on a hill, and looked down to see a beautiful green carpet covering the earth, on which the houses stood proudly. Whitewashed toilets, a couple of yards from each homestead, gave a finishing touch. As I got closer to the homes, I heard laughter echo in the air and saw little ones with bright eyes and pitch black shining faces running about happily with their friends, giving a final picture of resurrection and life.

I have not had the opportunity to find out how many husbands returned to their revitalised homesteads – the new life achieved through their wives' efforts whilst they were pushed to 'desert' their loved ones by the noxious migrant labour legislation.

The scenes which flashed on British television screens in 1985 when over 15,000 black miners, who had demanded a wage increase, were summarily dismissed from work and sent home, come alive in my mind. I was moved with compassion from a distance of 6,000 miles. These men were making legitimate demands through their newly established officially recognised National Union of Mineworkers. Their wages for doing such a dangerous job over generations were never assessed on the same basis as those of their counterparts, the white workers, who lived with their families in houses built by the mine owners.

Is it surprising that diseases like kwashiorkor and other

poverty-related diseases surface in the black communities in South Africa? Today there is much talk about 'Operation Hunger', a project established to combat the 'Ethiopia condition' in South Africa. The answer to all the problems in this country will not be solved by 'Operation Hunger' and similar programmes, but by the complete dismantling of apartheid; opening doors for black people to participate in the decision-making processes, as well as sharing equally the wealth and the land of the country so that every person in South Africa may derive the maximum benefit from all their efforts and contributions to the society.

Women at work, Ukhula

LET THEM EAT PINEAPPLES!

Liseka Mda

I never thought I would see the day when my children would sleep with nothing but water in their stomachs. Poverty has always been foreign to me. It happened to other people. Unfortunate people like Notobile, Notayimile and Nolayini, who do not have husbands. Notobile's and Nolayini's husbands are dead. Notayimile's has been confined to a mental hospital for years. The village understands their poverty, and they give them this and that every now and then. Rere's wife gives them clothes for their children. But then, things are bad now. People are not so eager to part with food or money like before. Especially for someone like me, who has a husband.

It has taken the village longer than it has taken me to accept that I am no longer well off by the village's standards. People used to come to me to borrow money, maize, everything. Now, I owe the whole village. Gone are the days when I would have spare cash in case ... and I could get things on credit from Rere's shop because I was considered one of his best customers. Nowelile has been on my back for her two tin cans of maize for a long time. Some people do not greet me any more. I can't even look them in the eye. Cups of sugar, tea, powdered soap, tin cans of flour, maize meal, uncountable litres of paraffin, and of course money. I owe it all. I do not want to think about the money I owe Rere for groceries. It is over R300 now, and he is not giving me groceries any more. Who would?

How can I pay it all back? I have tried to sell fat cakes to the schoolchildren, but the principal recently kicked all sellers off the school gates. I had decided to stop anyway because the children just did not have the money to buy. I have tried helping people when they are planting, hoeing or reaping maize, but the little money I get from that is not enough to feed my children. It kills

110

me to see them trying to be brave for me. Poor things do not even know that you cannot be brave when you are hungry. I have sat down and thought and I have decided I must go and look for a job.

Novumile, my best friend, told me everything was going to be all right. It was convenient to believe her. Talk about not being realistic. Well, this is the third year, and things have gone steadily worse. I owe Novumile most of all. My debt to her is more than financial. If it were not for her moral support, I would have been forced to leave my children much earlier than this. She has fed me and my children all this time. Her husband would kill her if he knew how much of his money has come our way. After all I am not his wife, am I? So we have decided that it would be better for me to find a job now. Of course we fought a lot before coming to that agreement, but she has eventually accepted that I have to go. I think in her heart of hearts she has known all along. It's just that she feels very protective of me. She is also going to be very lonely with me gone. I do not want to think about life in a big city without my children, and most importantly without Novumile. She has volunteered to look after my children when I am gone. Who would have thought that the events of one day could alter the lives of so many women so dramatically?

It all started five years ago. One summer morning, I was getting ready to go to the fields because weeds had been waging a relentless war against my maize for weeks. For a change there was cool weather, and it was obvious that we would all have a good time in the fields. My field was on the slopes facing the east, and with its green leaves waving to the sky, it was considered one of the best. The drought had been with us for two years, but my field could still yield a reasonable crop. That was another time. I have a dry patch of ground for a field now of course.

I was saying we were getting ready to go when there was a knock at the door. It was Mchontso, the headman's messenger. He told us the headman had called a meeting of the village. The headman wanted to report on his journey to the chief's place. I don't really care what he does and where he goes. I have reason to believe that he is a stupid old thing. Not because he is married to the best witch in the village, and I have that on good authority – Novumile's – but the fact that Rere thinks he is stupid *does* make him stupid. I have confidence in everything Rere says.

Rere is our shopkeeper, and Novumile tells me that he is very educated. She says he is one of the few people who have done all the standards there are at school. Before Novumile told me about his education, I thought the people with the best education were nurses, because they had passed standard 10. Now Novumile tells me Rere has gone beyond the 13th standard. So I asked her what he was doing in a village shop if he could be a doctor. And she said it was the best he could do so as not to get himself arrested, because he had been a pain to the government when he lived in the capital.

On this particular day, I was very cross with the government and its headman. It is difficult to get people to help one hoe the fields. People who are good with the hoe, like Nolayini, are booked well in advance. I had managed to get her and a few women to help me. And on top of that, the sun was hiding behind clouds, the ideal weather for spending the whole day in the fields. And the headman had to choose that day for a meeting!

Novumile thought we should go to the meeting because the headman was the agent of the government. At least that was true, because he is definitely not our agent. I don't even know how he got to be headman. It was one of those things that happen overnight. Our old headman, who was a sweet man, had died. Before we had wiped our eyes, Maqoqo was headman. Rere says the chief put him there because he is a fool. Anyway, we went to the meeting. The headman has three big huts which are arranged in a triangle. When there is a meeting we sit in the space between the huts and the kraal. There we found Maqoqo and two other men I did not recognize, facing the group of men and women from the village.

Shortly afterwards, Moqoqo stood up and said: 'Countrymen, I have called you to report on my meeting with the chief last week. As some of you may remember, I was asked by this village to take our complaint about the boys from Makwayini. The chief was very sympathetic to our problem. He even asked his wife to bring us a tin can of beer. Now you all know that the chief is not very generous with his beer. He likes it better when

112

we brew for *him*. But he did share his beer with *me*. I have not tasted better beer in years! It would do the whole village a lot of good if our wives could improve their brewing skills. And I told the chief so. He said maybe the maize harvest was not so good in this village. I told him we were not relying on the harvest, seeing that it has been poor for years now. I told the chief that we were buying our maize from Rere. I was right there, wasn't I? So the chief said maybe we should stop buying maize from Rere. It was possible that he was selling us poor quality maize to make a huge profit for himself.'

He had hardly finished the sentence when Vangembali shot up. 'Now wait a minute Maqoqo. We are not here to listen to Maqanderhamba's nonsense. He is just a fool who spends his non-sleeping hours in town getting drunk. He can't tell us anything about Rere. We all know that Rere is the best thing that has ever happened to this village. It does not matter why he came here in the first place. He sells his goods really cheap, cheaper even than the shops in town. Now where have you ever heard of such a thing? He is unlike some of the shopkeepers around, including Futhayo, the one this chief of yours is trying to force down our throats. And it's only because they belong to the same clan. Futhayo is a greedy thing, selling his bag of maize for R50 while Rere is selling for R38.50. People travel from the sea to buy a bag of maize from Rere. Doesn't that say something about Rere's prices? And it is good quality maize. Even when there was a shortage of maize, we were getting a good deal from Rere. Do you remember the time when he bought poor quality maize? As soon as people told him that it was of poor quality, he took whatever maize remained from everyone, and returned it to the wholesalers, getting good maize for all of us. And he explained to us that the rotten maize was sent by America, because the boers in the Orange Free State were not producing enough. Didn't he explain all this to us? Well I'll tell you now that he did. And we have never had the misfortune of eating poor quality maize again. America can keep his maize.

'Of course Maqanderhamba does not like Rere because he won't lick his arse, Rere refuses to pay all the money we are forced to pay when Maqanderhamba journeys to the capital, Springtown, and when all those government people from Springtown visit this district of ours. So, all in all, Rere is not

113

their fool, and they know it. But the point is, we are not here to discuss maize and beer making.'

A lot of heads were being nodded now. At this stage old man Khubalo stood up. His voice made a very eerie sound when he spoke. I always thought listening to him gave one an idea of the kind of speech one's ears are going to hear after death. He was older than everybody in the village. My father, when he was still alive, used to tell me that even when he was a young man, Khubalo was the oldest person in the village. Novumile thinks it is a good thing to live forever, and I have been trying to convince her that it is not. So much is changing now. That it is not for the best is known even by the most stupid person. I don't really want to be here when it gets worse. Novumile says she would like to see it all when the world changes. One more argument not resolved.

Anyway, Khubalo stood up at the meeting and everyone shooshed everyone else. 'That's true my son. The problem here is those boys from Makwayini. In the past four months, they have killed two boys from this village. In the old days we would have dismissed the thing and told the boys to fight back. But the fact is, our boys are younger than those Makwayini boys and we cannot send them to their deaths. We have done the best we can by putting a stop to our boys going to the same dances with the Makwayini boys, but we cannot always be sure our boys won't go. It is even possible those boys could waylay our boys at night when they are making their endless journeys. Journeys, we cannot say anything about. Boys must have their fun, as long as the girls are not complaining. We made our own journeys in our young days and our parents never asked us about them!

'Of course none of you know anything about my parents. But I can assure you they were parents just like you. Now as parents you are concerned that the Makwayini boys are bothering the Christian children on their way back from school. I am not a Christian. I was born too early for it, and the rest of you here who are not Christians, you have your reasons. But the Christians who are here are worried about the safety of their children. Some have even gone so far as to blame us because the quarrel started at a non-Christian dance. They say they have to suffer because of the actions of non-Christians. That bothers me. I wear my red blankets because I have always worn them, and my father before me wore them, not because I am a fool. Those men who wear trousers and jackets have their reasons which do not concern me. We have always lived in harmony in this village, Christians and non-Christians. And I don't think stupid boys should divide us. Which is why I am taking a keen exception to Moqoqo's treating this matter carelessly, telling us about beer. Now I will ask you Maqoqo. What did Qandalerhamba say about our problem?' And with that, Khubalo sat down.

Maqoqo has a tendency to sweat. I have always believed that one does not sweat when there is no sun, at least not in the face, unless one has something to hide. Whatever it was that Maqoqo was trying to hide must have been heavy, like the stones Rere uses to weigh our maize. He was sweating profusely now. He may be a cunning old thing but the truth does throw him off balance.

'Now do ... do ... don't ge ... get me wrong. I did not forget what I had to tell the king, I beg your pardon, the chief. I even told him that some kids were not going to school for fear of the Makwayini boys. Of course that's not entirely accurate, but before you tell me so, I want you to know that I wanted to make sure the chief would do something. He was a bit tipsy, you see. Let me come to the point now. The chief said he would do as we had asked, and contact the chief at Makwayini. He even said he would suggest to the Makwayini chief that he sends the troublesome boys to TEBA,[1] so that they could go to Johannesburg, and out of people's hair. I was very happy to hear that, I can assure you. There is nothing like a stint in the mines to tame wild boys.

'But the chief had something else to tell us. He said the government was introducing a new development scheme. He said ours was the first village to be considered for the new scheme because we were special to him. I do not make any trouble for him. Isn't that good news now?'

'Bad news most probably,' Khubalo muttered, 'and the fool does not even realize it.'

But Maqoqo continued: 'The chief said our district was one of the few that still had houses and fields in the same area. That was backward, he said. And he asked me if I liked being

[1] Temporary Employment Bureau of Africa

115

backward. I told him in no uncertain terms that I didn't, and I'm sure the same applies to you here. So the chief said we were going to re-arrange the village. And he said he would send two gentlemen from the government offices who would explain the details of the re-arrangement to us. As you can see, there are two gentlemen you don't know among us. Well I'll tell you. These gentlemen are the two men the chief promised to send us. A man of his word, the chief is, if you don't mind my saying so.'

One of the men stood up at this stage. He looked like he was the same age as Maqoqo. Maqoqo already had five grand-children then, and one of them had started school that same year. This man started speaking. I can't really tell you what he was saying because he was speaking English, but the other one stood up as well and spoke in Xhosa after every time the other man spoke. Novumile whispered to me that the one was repeating in Xhosa what the other was saying in English. At least I could hear it was Xhosa though he was using very difficult words. I'm sure no one heard the other man because even Siventshu who has worked in Cape Town for many years said afterwards that he could not follow that guy at all. Apparently the interpreter could follow him because he started speaking.

'Ladies and gentlemen. We are here today to bring you good news. Both of us work for the Department of Agriculture and Land Tenure. He says he is Ezekiel Kenkebe and I am Archibald Kuzile. We have been sent by the government. There are some people who would like you to believe that the government is not doing anything for you. One of them lives in this part of the country, but I won't mention any names. That's not why we are here. We are here to talk about non-biodegradable-orderly-habitation. For those of you who do not know that, it is a sophisticated form of agriculture and land settlement. This is a concept His Royal Highness, the State President of our prosperous country, KwaNtsokolo, King Fobela Ngxowa dis-covered when he visited Israel. That's another thing people do not realize, the importance of His Excellency's visits abroad.

'He goes to these places to tell the people who live there about our independent country, KwaNtsokolo. People do not know about our country because troublemakers like the ANC have been making mischief, telling overseas countries that our country is a puppet state that is being propped up by the government in

South Africa. Now, I am asking you, ladies and gentlemen, who is propping who? Don't we give SA men to work on the mines and other places? I am talking about the husbands of some of the women here. But do you know what SA does to your husbands? He lets them go crazy all over the place. They strike, and do all sorts of other things that communists do. They kill each other and lose their jobs. Is that what you want to happen to your husbands and sons?' He paused and looked around. He should have waited three years to ask me *that* question. There is a lot I could tell him now about what I would like to happen to my husband, but there was nothing then. There were a lot of elders who could have answered for all of us, but they decided to shut their mouths.

So the man continued: 'No, you don't want that to happen to them and we know that. That is why you don't hear of any strikes here in KwaNtsokolo. No unions! And that is the best thing we have ever done. To ban unions. No troubles at all. But of course SA won't admit the fact that we are cleverer than they are. But a lot of countries abroad believe us. That is why His Highness visits them every now and then. They believe that we are a sovereign state here. We manufacture toothpicks and sacks. How can we not be a sovereign state when we manufacture such important things? Of course you don't know what toothpicks are. If you knew, then you would know that, were it not for them even the South African State President would find it difficult to make his numerous speeches because of foreign bodies in his mouth. I won't go into sacks, you all know them.

'And I can assure you, this economic prosperity does bring countries to their senses as far as our country is concerned. That is why we have so many friends in the free world. The USA, Britain, Austria, Taiwan and Israel are our friends. You will all know of course that the children of our cabinet ministers and of other prominent citizens in this country are studying in Austria and the USA. This helps to strengthen our relations with these countries, Austria has sold us tractors and buses that are very advanced, technologically. Our army is making terrific use of the buses, and you will be able to use the tractors as well when the planting season is here. When His Excellency visits these countries, he is treated like the prodigal son. And do not forget that these are big important white men. That is why they gave him the secrets of this new non-biodegradable-habitation. Which is where I started.

'So, ladies and gentlemen, we bring you a system which has been perfected in Israel. Those of you who are Christians will know that this signifies great things. Which is why my lord considered the system in the first place. It will make people's lives very easy. There will be no more hunger for people because a lot of land will be available for cultivation. All in all, ladies and gentlemen, some of you are going to have to move. We have made a thorough study of this area, so we know what we are talking about. All the families that are living to the west of those two kissing hills, south of the grounds of the shop, will have to move to the vacant plots north of the shop. The whole area to the south of the shop will be converted into fields. All those who want new sites should assemble here on Monday next week. That's all, ladies and gentlemen.'

Was there confusion after that speech! People started speaking all at once but I'm sure they did not expect to be answered. The two gentlemen got into their white government car and drove off. People wanted to know where they were going to get money to build new homes. But as usual, it was left to Khubalo to voice our fears.

'Hey Maqoqo, what exactly are you up to?'

'You don't understand at all Khubalo. This is good for the village. When I was with the chief, he showed me photographs of places with schemes like this in other countries. There were green valleys everywhere, and people had food to eat.'

'I do not have any problems with green valleys that are in photographs. But you should know that we have not seen any green valleys here for a long time. I am also not against change, as long as it is good for us. I have lived long enough to know that things change. Maybe this is for the better as you say. But what I cannot understand is how you could let those two men leave without answering some questions about this scheme. For instance I want to know where we are going to get the money to build new homes.'

'I am sure the government will make a plan.'

'And how much do you know about that plan?'

'Of course I have not been told, but the chief will let me know when there is something to know.'

118

'We have to know now, Maqoqo. How are we going to choose plots if we do not know where we are going to get the money to develop those plots? I guess there's nothing you are going to tell us. It's just that sometimes I forget how stupid you are.' And the people dispersed after that.

I must say people's minds were already in the future. No one was waiting for Monday to choose plots. People were saying where they wanted to settle. Nowelile and Nokhamblish wanted to build their homes on the plots near the shop. That was only fair, because they always have money to spend. I certainly did not want any of those plots, and thank God I never got one. That would have meant living near Nowelile. I have never met a meaner or stingier person in all my life. All I wanted was to live near Novumile. Novumile already lived in the area north of the shop because she is a Christian, and this was mainly a Christian area. I did get the plot next to Novumile, and I'll be eternally grateful to my ancestors for looking after me this way. I don't know what I would have done without Novumile in these past three years.

But we did not have problems then. We were busy making jokes. Everybody was saying now was the time for Notobile to move. She had a legitimate excuse at last. Notobile has been living in a lone hut for years. I won't say anything about her being too lazy to even mix mud to keep it in a good condition. I just cannot understand how she can live in the only hut at the edge of a forest that is known to harbour everything belonging to the devil – ghosts, *iimpundulu*,[2] and the devil knows what other evil things he keeps in that forest. Notobile lives all alone in that hut. It was better when her husband was still alive, but now he's gone and her son has not come home for more than eight years. Notobile should have moved from that hut ages ago. It takes her a while to get to the nearest house. The only place she is close to is the shop. Much good that would do her if the inhabitants of the forest decided to visit her, because Rere locks his gates at night. I mean you walk with your heart virtually in your throat when you are walking alone to the shop, because one never knows what is going to happen. And that is during the day! Now, how about living next to that forest day and night?

[2]Witchcraft birds

119

Some people have even suggested that she is in league with the mentioned inhabitants. But I think she refuses to make the big decision, which is to move. Especially because she knows that is what everyone expects of her. Notobile won't do what is expected of her, no matter what. She said her hut was neither to the north nor the south of the shop, but to its east. She is still living there.

The joke is on me now of course. But it was on Notobile then, and we were both laughing when Novumile and I entered the shop. There was no customer inside. Rere was sitting in the office reading a book. I like it when the shop is empty. Then Rere can go on and on about the evils of places we will never see. As soon as we entered, he came through to the serving area. We greeted him, and after his customary 'Heke makhosikazi',[3] he started with questions.

'What did that mickey mouse have to say today?' I don't know what mickey mouse means, but I know who Rere refers to by it because the first time he said it, I asked him what he meant and he said he was referring to 'that baboon Maqoqo'. I let Novumile answer for both of us. You never know what Rere is going to say or do, so it is always wise to be cautious.

'Yeyele,[4] Rere.' She has always been dramatic. 'Maqoqo brought us two government men to tell us everyone who is living south of the shop is going to move to our area.'

'Why?'

'Because they are going to make this the Promised Land. Just like Israel.'

'God save the world from the United States and Israel! But really, is that what they told you?'

'Well we cannot be sure, can we? We have to rely on what the man who was speaking Xhosa told us. And I have known interpreters to lie. Don't they Rere?'

'What are you talking about? What's this thing about Xhosa? Is there another language spoken in this village?'

'The other man was speaking English.'

'The hypocrites! Why speak English in a village that is at the

---

[3] 'Good day matrons' – very respectful.
[4] In full it means, 'The cow is sunk into a swampy piece of ground.' But the shortened version used here means, 'Things are bad.'

end of the world? Do you know that in their little aeroplanes they speak Xhosa?'

'Oh!'

'Yes they do. They want to impress the whites who use the planes, "See, we have our own language here, we do not need yours, thank you very much," while all the time they use it to address people who do not understand a word of it! But tell me about this moving business. What are they going to do with the land to the south then?'

'It is going to be all fields so that everybody can have land to cultivate.'

'I am sure "everybody" does not include you, you lazy thing!'

'Nothing will ever get me to the fields, never! My father-in-law went to his grave with that noble knowledge. It has taken his son longer to realize it though.'

'So what is going to happen to the old homesteads?'

'My guess is they will have to pull them down. You can't just make it easy for the ghosts,' I joined in.

'Who is going to pay for the new homes?'

'I'll tell you Rere. They did not say it, but I can assure you we are going to pay through our noses to live in those new homes. Mark my words. After dropping the bombshell, those two men jumped into their car and drove off like a pair of criminals, which could be what they are.'

'Did they say why the move was necessary in the first place?'

'It is a development scheme. That's what they said.'

'Well, I'll tell you something Nowandile, you must be very suspicious of anyone who uses that word. "Development" is the most misused word I have come across. Botha kicks people out of their homes to build homes for whites. And do you know what he calls that? "Development". The government of this bantustan sucks all of us dry to finance a "Development" Corporation that works against us and buys businesses for their sons and daughters. Don't tell me about "development".'

A few people came into the shop just then. So Novumile and I went home.

A lot has happened since that day. Khubalo never made it to the new area. He died before the year was out. I think things started to deteriorate then. Suddenly a lot of things were happening and there was no one to ask the questions for us. For a start, we never got any compensation for our homes. We had to fork out a lot of money for building material. Poor Rere tried to sell building material as cheaply as possible, but building material is expensive anyway. And there is the drought – it hasn't given us any breathing space at all. Cattle have died. That means hard times during the planting season.

It was Rere who reminded us about the tractors the government had promised us. The rest of us had long forgotten about them. So Maqoqo was asked to take two men and to go and ask for help from the chief. Maqanderhamba said we could only have the use of the tractors if every house in the village paid R10. So we paid. Those who did not have the money borrowed, so that the whole village paid up. But the tractors never came. Of course they did come to plough Maqanderhamba's fields, and we thought they would come later for us lesser beings. But that was all.

Seeing that Maqoqo was doing nothing, we asked Rere to go to the government offices for us. Normally he doesn't want anything to do with the government but, poor soul, he could see that we were desperate. So he went. Rere's report shocked all of us, except veteran pessimists like Novumile, who said we believed anything that drifted past our ears. Rere said the government officers at the Land Tenure office had told him it was not possible for us to get the tractors because our land was all slopes, and the road to our village was in a bad state. They could not risk breaking the tractors for a small village like ours. And whatever he said, even mentioning the R10, they would not budge. Maybe Rere was not the right person to send, but who else would have gone? The thing about sloping land was news to us, because private tractors do come to our fields, when they are paid to do so, with no trouble at all.

The thing about the road was not news at all. Have we suffered because of that road! For all of the fifteen years that Rere has been here, the government has done nothing to maintain that road. Caterpillars and all the trucks that work on the roads drive past the junction to our village every year. Maybe they think they'll fix Rere that way. But he is as stubborn as ever. They are fixing us instead. We cannot get bread when it has rained because the bakery truck won't drive when there is mud. Rere says the baker is 'in league with all those thieves in the capital' because the wholesale truck and Rere in his rickety old van do drive on that road. Rere says he will eventually have to buy bread from Loitertown, a town which is farther away. Goodbye fresh bread.

But who would have known that, because of the events of that memorable day, I would lose my husband? The thing is, I did get the plot next to Novumile's. But I got a few more neighbours as well. Nowam was one of them. I have nothing against Nowam. She is just a gossip, nothing more. But I hate her husband's, Nomeva's guts. He has always been a rogue. And as soon as we moved in, he struck up a friendship with my husband. I could not understand it. I had always thought my husband was a good judge of personality. It just goes to show that we don't know our men. As soon as he had Nomeva as a friend, he would go to town every day when he was home for the holidays. That meant spending lots of money. There is nothing else you can do in our little dusty town. For a while I found the friendship amusing. Nomeva had funny stories to tell about Johannesburg all the time. Of course it is not so funny now that the same Johannensburg has swallowed my husband.

I had grown up thinking Jo'burg was a terrible place for one to live in. There were always stories about robbers, rapists and murderers. But from Nomeva's stories, I would picture Johannesburg as a beautiful place, with educated people and Christian dances every night. Beautiful, shiny cars would drive up and down minding their own business. I'm sure Nomeva fed my husband more glowing stories on their trips to town. These days I've formed my own picture of Johannesburg. Whenever I think of the place, which is all the time really, I see this huge dragon, with scales, long fangs and bat wings. There are women under the wings who are very beautiful, but have claws with which they attach themselves to people's husbands.

Recently, I have added another image to this picture. Rere is responsible for that. A few weeks ago, I accompanied Novumile to the shop. There were quite a few people in the shop. Rere was his usual bright self. He was teasing Notobile about her maize crop. Everyone's maize was dry because of the drought, but Notobile's field was consistently red because of weeds. After a while, he stopped and came to serve us. Novumile had come to do her monthly shopping, much to the envy of us all because she can spend more than R100 on groceries at one go. Everyone was saying how fortunate she was to have a husband who sent her money every month.

'By the way, where does your husband work?' Rere asked her.

'Johannesburg.'

'Where exactly in Johannesburg?'

'In Nigel.'

'*Maye babo*!'[5] Rere shrieked. 'He is right in thick of it, isn't he?'

'In the thick of what, Rere?'

'Riots. Five people have died so far. The police force is responsible for three of those, the other two have died in the clashes between the migrant hostel dwellers and the township residents.'

'My God Rere, do you think Mvuzo's father is safe there?'

'No one is safe in this world we live in Novumile. You have to accept that. But relax, your husband's name was not mentioned. I'm sorry I started this.'

But he had started it all the same, and everyone in the shop was open-mouthed with shock. Rere's stories have that effect on people. Me, I was just sorry my husband did not work in Nigel. I could just imagine him being stabbed by residents. He would stagger with blood all over him directly into the fire of the policemen. He would fall, and they would load him into a car, and drive him to the hospital. He would die before the car could even reach the hospital, trying to say my name. He would die a frustrated man because he wouldn't be able to tell them, to tell me, that he was sorry he had abandoned us, and that I should fetch the plough he lent to Mvolovu against my will, three years ago. Rere says I am much too bitter for my own good. He says I am laying all the blame on my husband while I should save quite a substantial amount for the system that is responsible for my husband being alone in Johannesburg in the first place.

I know differently. It was no system that took my husband away from me. It was a woman. She and my husband are to blame for all the suffering I have been through. Of course Nomeva has to share some of the blame, seeing that he is the one who dragged my husband away from Cape Town to

[5] 'Oh my!'

124

Johannesburg in the first place. They did try to convince me that we would all benefit from the move. My husband would send more money because the mines paid much more than the Cape Town docks. I tried to dissuade him from going. Something was telling me it was not a good move, but of course I could not say why. Nomeva made fun of me, saying anybody who listened to a woman's intuition in this day and age was a fool. So they ignored me. I would have liked for my intuition to be wrong just this once, but I am sorry to report that I was right, again. When my husband was working in Cape Town, he would send me R150 every second month. When he first went to Johannesburg, he used to send me R200 every two months. This went on for two years. I was one of the few women in the village who had a steady income. Then he started taking longer to send money. And when it got here, it would be R120, then R90, and the last time he sent something, it was R40. What he thought I would do with R40, I don't know. I am sure he did not know either because there wasn't even the customary note telling me about the hardship in Johannesburg, and how to spend the money.

Maybe he has finally realized that I know that he is lying to me. I know that he is living with a woman and her three children, plus two of their own. Well, lucky them. My children have not seen their father for three years, and from the look of things, they will never see him again. Novumile and I were arguing about him a few weeks ago.

'You are just a coward. Why don't you take your children and go to Johannesburg? You have got to bring that man to his senses,' she screamed at me.

'Maybe I am a coward because I just don't see myself crossing a million rivers for a man who is obviously not interested in me,' I screamed back.

'You are just a proud peacock. You just won't bend that arrogant neck of yours.'

'I would rather be a proud peacock than a wet hen, which is what going to Johannesburg would reduce me to.'

Suddenly the match was over. I am sure both of us were thinking about Nozinzile. Several years ago, the news that her husband was living with a woman in East London arrived in our village. There is just no way you won't hear about such a thing. People who come back from the cities bring all sorts of news when they come home. Good or bad, it does not matter. That's how I found out about my husband, and it was the same with Nozinzile as well. She did bring back her husband. But for the life of me, I can't see any good that has done her. She is stuck with a non-working husband who plays at being a carpenter, while she is running around the whole district buying pigs to slaughter and sell. I think she would have been better off with him in East London. She would still be running after screaming pigs, but she would only have her own and her children's stomachs to feed.

Novumile says it does not have to be like that for me. But she does not know what it will be like, and I am not curious enough to want to find out. Let's say I do persuade him to come back home. And then what will I do with him? Who says he will get a job in Cape Town now? Everybody is saying how bad things are in the cities. There are many men in the village who have not worked for years. No thanks, he can stay in Johannesburg. And I will go to East London.

Novumile has finally accepted that I am going to East London, and not Johannesburg. Now the argument is about the job I will be doing. I want to work on the pineapple farms, and she says that is a bit low for me, why don't I look for a kitchen job in the white areas? Sometimes she forgets that I only went as far as Standard 1, and not Standard 7 like her. What on earth would I do in a white woman's kitchen? What about English? Never! It's definitely pineapples for me.

Servant's quarters

AMAPHEKULA (Terrorist)

Fatima Meer

The road to Ulundi passes through lush cane fields and fruit orchards and exotic tibushinas and bougainvilleas. The town centre of Eshowe is a symphony of superb architecture and tropicana. The valleys stretch across hundreds of miles, exquisitely patchworked in fruit orchards and cane fields, dark green and light, that catch the gleam of the morning sun as it ripples through the sprinkling waters that keep the fields nourished.

Every now and then this idyllic splendour is pierced by a fragment of Kwa-Zulu – hard soil and thorn bushes undulating over thousands of difficult, uncultivatable hills. No border post or signs proclaim the transition from the Republic to Kwa-Zulu, but the signs are all there – the scarred earth, the dry dust, the shale, the sudden disappearance of trees.

The bridge across the White Umfolozi is treacherous – the river is a bed of mud and stones. But it is not always like that. When the storms break, the rain waters rush and burst the banks. Two bridges have been washed away and their concrete clogs up the river bed. Across the river, and above, rise the flat, white houses of Ulundi, and apart from these, from a treeless waste expensively fenced in concrete, rises Parlamende, as the locals say it, the Parliament of Chief Buthelezi. Close by are the houses of the members, grand by local standards, and opposite these, 'The Smallest Holiday Inn in the World.'

One needs to pass through all this before one turns into the dirt road that leads to Phangode and Dayeni where Khathazile and Salusha have their kraals, and one invariably coughs through the dust that other vehicles churn up and throw into your face. The only delivery vehicle one is likely to encounter along the way is a beer truck.

The police said that Mzamo Zulu brought the *amaphekula* (terrorists) here because of the *ihlathi* (forest), in which they

128

could hide, but there is only a sparse scattering of *isinqwa* (thorn trees) and *mhlaba* (aloes) which hide nothing.

Salusha and Khathazile had spent a year in detention, and had been found guilty of harbouring terrorists. They left the court for their cells bemused and uncomprehending how this should have happened to them. In a week's time they would be brought to the magistrate for sentencing, and their council had to plead in mitigation so that their innocence would be punished less severely, for innocent they were.

Salusha, who had long passed his eightieth birthday, without having known a single one, was the king's *induna*; Khathazile was his adopted daughter.

The approach to Dayeni is heralded by the district store – where trucks and combis stop, and passengers alight to quench the great thirst that builds up in the hot, waterless, scrub country. The store looks like nothing on the outside, but it is well stocked within, mostly with cooked and uncooked foods and soft drinks. It also provides music, to which the younger, weary travellers, but more usually the locals, step into a breezy staccato dance.

Opposite the store is the Phangode market – some three or four women vendors and twice as many hangers-on, squatting under the trees, selling vegetables and fruit, and when the police do not look, beer. Khathazile had been one of the vendors, before her arrest, an attractive, well-proportioned woman in her early forties. Like her fellow vendors she has never been to school, but like them, she could count her change and calculate her profit. She had recently introduced a new line in the market, clothing – blouses and shirts, that had hung colourfully from an improvised rail, strung across two branches of a tree.

Khathazile had lived an easy-going, merry life in that area until her arrest. She had gone through three steadies and numerous itinerants. She needed the latter to support the children left by the former. She had four children, and 13-year-old Mhlepheni, her daughter, was her eldest. But men were nt her mainstay, she supported her family largely on the small business she conducted at the Phangode market.

Home for Khathazile was the three huts that she and her common-law husband, Hlongwane had built on his land; the first to sleep in, the second for receiving guests and for sleeping the children, and the third for cooking. She had dug a fire-place at the centre of the third hut both for cooking and heating. Hlongwane had put in the wattle poles. She had built the walls with empty beer cartons and mud. He had put in the two windows, and glazed them; she had put in the doors and the third window which had no glass and which they covered with a cloth. The huts are in ruins now. Soon after their arrest, hers and Salusha's, attackers had come and burnt down her huts and the huts of Tholakele, Salusha's daughter-in-law whose kraal adjoined hers. They would never know who had done the deed, but it was not the people in their area.

Salusha had served as *induna* for the last ten years. Before him, his elder brother was *induna*, and before his elder brother, his father, and before his father, his grandfather. Salusha was now 85 years old and he had known three kings: the present King Zwelithini, who had appointed him, his father, Cyprian, and his grandfather, Solomon. King Solomon had given him his regiment and it was during his time, when Hitler warred in Europe and dragged the whole world into his war, that he had taken his first wife, Ma Omkhulu. Life had been good to him. He had married six more wives, and raised a large kraal of sons and daughters and countless grandchildren. His *isibaya* was full of cattle. He had sons who worked in town and his youngest boy was going to school in Kwa-Mashu. He himself had never been to school, neither had his older sons, but times were changing.

One morning towards the latter part of the year – Salusha did not reckon time according to the European calendar, but according to seasons for ploughing and sowing and reaping – Mzamo Zulu had come to visit him. Mzamo was always welcome at his kraal. He had been resting in his hut, when the women had called out that there were visitors to see him and his hut had darkened and Mzamo had stooped to enter through the low door. He had said he was with Magula, whom Salusha did not know. Mzamo had been in no hurry to broach his business, but had finally come round to it. He told Salusha that he had two people who needed a site to set up a kraal. They were his people, good people, and he wanted the *induna* to allocate a site for them.

Salusha had no hesitation in granting the request. Mzamo had rights in the area and these rights extended to his relatives.

Moreover he was the king's man. He had known him to drive the king around and to bring him messages from the king. He readily agreed to give him a site. He called for his son Michael to show him what was available. Salusha had known that at the time of that visit, Mzamo had no longer been working for the king, but that had not altered his respect for him, for he had known that he was still very much the king's friend and that he visited the royal kraal freely and was welcome there. But he had fallen out of favour with the *umntwana*, Chief Buthelezi. They said he had criticised the *umntwana*. Salusha was not present when it had happened, but he had heard that Mzamo had been summoned to Nongoma, and in the presence of the councillors, the *umntwana* had told Mzamo that he did not wish to see his face in his mother's place, Princess Magogo, the daughter of King Dinizulu.

Once the *umntwana* spoke, no one else could speak, not even the king could question him. The *umntwana* had become greater than the king. that was the white people's doing. Never before had a chief minister been greater than the king. He remembered the time with a pain that was as sharp now as it had been then, when the *umntwana* had summoned the king before parliament and accused him of plotting against him and scolded him like a child before the whole assembly. They had all smarted under the humiliation. Then the king, much younger then and very inexperienced, had run out of the assembly, and Salusha and all those who had accompanied him, had run with him, as tradition had required of them.

It was not for commoners to concern themselves with the quarrels of royalty, and Salusha had a reputation for being discreet, but he also had a reputation for being straightforward and honest, and when it was indiscreet to speak out to others one could still speak to one's self and he had told himself then, that the chief minister was too overbearing. But this had not prevented him from becoming a member of Inkatha and when Chief Buthelezi had sent his minister, Khanyile, to his district, he had called all the kraal heads together and persuaded them to pay their membership fees. He had paid R20, for himself and for his wives, and his sons had paid on their own behalf. He did not know what Inkatha did or what they got from Inkatha. He knew what the king did, that he shared his wealth with them. When

131

they organized the reed ceremony of the young women, and collected cattle, the king gave twice as much from his *isibaya*.

It was a few months later, just before Christmas, that Mzamo returned with his people to take up his claim. He was surprised to see that the 'people' were mere boys, bright-eyed, pleasant-faced and well-spoken. However, he did not raise this with Mzamo. He had given him his word and they were now his problem. He listened patiently to Mzamo's instructions that he should protect the boys from the police. He assumed that there was probably something wrong with their passes – that did not disturb him; practically everybody needed some protection from the police; the laws of the state they represented were so different from their own laws in so many ways that many things that were necessary for his people were deemed illegal by the police.

When Mzamo left, Salusha sat down and talked to the two young men, introduced to him as Themba and Mpumelelo, about their families. They did not tell him much but they did admit that they were not married. He had suspected as much. So he told them that in that case he could not give them land to start their own kraal, but they were welcome to stay in his kraal, and he gave them a hut. If they were disappointed, they did not show it. They expressed their gratitude and told him that they would build him a hut, and they did, a very large and a very good hut, the best in his kraal, and they taught some of the young men how to build such huts.

Salusha became very fond of the young men. He did not sit and talk with them, or drink beer with them. That would have been quite out of order. But he saw how helpful they were and how popular they became with the local people. They were clever with their hands and their minds. They found small things and big that needed doing and they organised the young people to do it with them. They appeared to him to be inspiring a new spirit, especially among the jobless youth. The young men didn't hang around so listlessly any more. They appeared to have a sense of purpose. They jogged with Themba and Mpumelelo in the early mornings and in the evenings; they played football; they repaired the roads; they took an interest in his court and when it was in session under the tree sat quietly by and listened respectfully. He was so pleased with them that he recommended them to the people in all the eight neighbourhoods under his jurisdiction, and he told his sons that there was much he could learn from them.

He wondered in retrospect whether they had misunderstood him into thinking that he had wanted them to become *amaphekula*. It was only in court that he realised that Themba and Mpumelelo had had a great deal more to teach than he had imagined. They had gone about in that matter so quietly, and so cautiously, that he had known nothing about it. They had wanted the young men in the area to bear arms against the white government and they had, according to the police, enticed several young men in his area, including his two young sons.

But at the time he had fondly thought how good it would be if they settled down permanantly in his district, and he could after all allocate the land Magula had chosen for them. And that was why he had been so disappointed, when after spending just six weeks in his kraal, they announced that they would be leaving to find employment. Salusha had sighed. That is how it was. One could never keep the young people to the land, and of course, if one did, one would starve. So it was right that they went to seek employment.

It happened soon after they had left. And however few the years left to Salusha, he is doomed to spend them in the memory of the terror of that night, and the terror that followed that night and continues with him to this day. In the pitchness and blackness of that night, the police surrounded his kraal and forced him and his entire family out of their sleeping mats and huts and questioned them about the strangers they were hiding. 'We have no strangers in our kraal,' he had insisted. He knew the police had a thing about strangers. They had told him to report strangers to them, and he had done so on the one occasion he had seen two white men in his area. It did not occur to him at first that they were referring to Themba and Mpumelelo. How could it? They were as his own sons. Besides they were no longer in the kraal. So he said again that there were no strangers in his kraal. That had made them very angry. They had not believed him. They had searched all the huts. They had kicked and sworn and then, to the shock and bewilderment of his people, had pushed him into their van and driven off with him.

It was a terrible thing to have happened to him in the presence of his people. He had called on Jehovah and prayed silently in his heart all the way.

They had driven to Nongoma where they had locked him in a cell, and for a day and a half they questioned him about the terrorists. They had kicked him and twisted his neck, and boxed him about his ears so that his teeth had rattled in his mouth and some had fallen out. They had made him pick up heavy objects and put these on his head, and stand with them for hours, until his legs had buckled and he had thought he would fall. They had struck him on his bare back with open hands until the skin had peeled, and they had gripped his forefinger between two sticks and squeezed until the blood had drained to the end and congealed under his nail. Such things had happened to him that it was not dignified to talk of all of them.

For all the assaults, and despite his age, Salusha had been like a bull through it all. 'Why are you assaulting me?' he had shouted. 'I am not a policeman. I am not an *impimpi*' (informer), and this had made the black policemen even angrier and one of them had said, 'I don't know why the king appointed this dog as *induna*.' The white policeman said they were going to kill him, and they had brought in a black box and said his coffin was ready to receive his body.

He had realised even before they had arrested him that they were looking for Themba and Mpumelelo, and he had begun to wonder what it was the boys had done, but with that wondering there had also developed in him a protective shield for them. He eventually told the police that there had been these two young men who had stayed a while in his kraal, but that they were as his sons, and no strangers, and very good boys. It was then that they released him.

By then he had been standing, sleepless, for a day and a half, and so exhausted he could barely hold himself together. They had said they were returning him to his kraal; he had shuffled to the van, struggled to climb in, and slumped into his seat, his eyes closing almost the same instant. He had not known when Khathazile had stopped the van and sat down beside him.

Salusha was as father to Khathazile. She had never known her father, and her mother had died in childbirth, so Salusha had taken her over and Ma Omkhulu had raised her. They had cared for her children too, until she had moved to Hlongwane's kraal.

So it was hardly surprising that Khathazile broke out into a wail when she saw Salusha in that condition, and had to be restrained by the police, who threatened to put her down that moment if she did not stop her whining.

It was pure chance that she had met up with Salusha. She had just returned from Durban and was walking down the street in Nongoma before taking a bus to Phangode when she had heard the policeman call her: 'Hey Kate. come here'. He had behaved as if she was his for the plucking: 'Why is your complexion so fair today?' he had asked, 'and where are you coming from?' Then he had asked her if Salusha was not her father and told her that they were taking him home, and if she hurried to the police station she could get a lift to Dayeni with him.

They had driven to Dayeni in a silence broken only by her occasional whimpering. Khathazile had got off at Phangode; the police vehicle had continued to Dayeni, where they had shaken Salusha out of his deep sleep, and dragged him out. All at once a great cry had rent his kraal as his wives and sons had come rushing to receive him. They supported him tenderly and laid him down in his hut and saw how he had been assaulted. Leaves were boiled and Ma Omkhulu had applied poultices wherever she could to cool his pain, and his eldest son had gone to the *inyanga* so that evil could be distanced from their kraal.

But the evil was travelling to Khathazile's kraal and she was completely unaware of it.

In the early hours of Saturday morning, by other reckoning – by Khathazile's it was the night that followed Friday – she was aroused from her sleep by a persistent knocking and calling at her window. When she opened the door she found Bafana, standing with a gun. Bafana was all right, but the gun startled her. What was he doing with a gun, that part of the night, outside her hut? He was only a child, Salusha's youngest son by his fifth wife, Zanele. Before he could say anything, she asked about the gun. 'Oh!' he said, 'it's just for shooting birds,' and then he told her that his father had sent him to her with two friends who were waiting outside. He requested that she should put them up for the night.

Khathazile could not refuse anything that Salusha asked her to do. He was both father and *induna*, so she said he could bring his friends, and they could sleep in the second hut, with the children. She went into the hut and took the children off the bed, and re-arranged them on the sleeping mats on the floor, and gave the bed to the visitors. Bafana introduced Themba and Mpumelelo, and she left the three sitting on the bed, and retired to her own hut, which she was sharing that night with other visitors.

Bafana was at the time schooling at Kwa-Mashu, and was on holiday at Phangode. He had met Themba and Mpumelelo during December at his father's kraal and had been highly impressed by them. He had felt good and important when they had asked him to join them with his elder brother, Michael, and his father, Councillor Kuphelokwakhe, to learn how to shoot. They had taught him to use a pistol. Apart from practising shooting, they had played football together and talked about the ANC, and freedom and dignity. He agreed with what they said, and was tremendously drawn to them. At daybreak, when Khathazile began her morning routine, she found the three young men sitting under the tree opposite her huts. She went into the hut they had occupied to make up the bed and found two guns folded in a sheet. It made her nervous and angry. She suspected Bafana had not been truthful to her. She called him and demanded an explanation. Who were those people? Were they thieves? Were they running away from anyone? He insisted that they were good people, they were *abelungisi* – they put things right. He said his father would not have sent them to her if they were otherwise. In any case, he assured her, they were leaving that day, and he and Themba were going to Pongolo to get a car.

She remained very unhappy with his explanation. She was thinking of the police who had come to Salusha's kraal and about Salusha'a detention. She decided to see Salusha about it, but when she reached his kraal, he was just leaving with some *umnumzane*. She knew better than to stop an *induna* in his tracks, so she went instead to Bafana's mother and reported the matter to her.

Zanele was agitated, particularly about the guns. 'They shouldn't walk around with guns,' she said. 'They should hide the guns in the cave where everyone hides their guns.' Khathazile explained that they were leaving that day. Zanele said it did not

136

matter when they left, the guns should not be in her house. It was dangerous to have them there. She shook her head and said the boys were too careless and that there was no excuse for it, particularly since what had happened to Salusha. Then she invited Khathazile to have some beer. Khathazile left soon after, with her children, to take a train to Mahlabathini to buy beer for her business.

At Mahlabathini she bumped into Bafana. He told her he was with Themba and they had missed the bus to Pongolo, so they would have to spend another day with her. 'One day!' she retorted. 'You know there is no bus on Sunday,' and then told him what his mother had said about the guns. He promised to remove them when he got back to Phangode.

Khathazile bought her beer and returned home with her children. Bafana and Themba returned a little later. It was dark by then. The boys said it was too hot in the hut, and they would sleep outside, under the tree; she gave them two blankets.

On Sunday morning, Hlongwane arrived. Khathazile was powdering herself in their bedroom. He drew a chair and sat beside her. Looking out of the window, he spied some heads and enquired about the strangers in the yard. She told him it was Bafana and his friends and called Bafana to explain. Bafana came with a gun and Hlongwane became more interested in the gun than the explanation. He examined it and enquired whether he could get one like that for himself. Bafana said he would give him one, which pleased him no end, so he asked Khathazile whether she had given the guests food. That angered her, and brought out her stock grievance against him, that he gave her no money, brought no food into the house and yet had the cheek to act the grand host. Hlongwane placated her, and the afternoon proceeded peacefully. The following morning, Khathazile walked him to the bus stop.

She felt far more relaxed about her gun-carrying visitors after Hlongwane had left, and almost forgot about them by the time Mandhlophe, her lover, came demanding her attention. They went to the local store, and had a little spree, drinking, eating chicken and jiving to some banjo strumming. They were both a little tipsy by the time they left the store and returned to her kraal.

Mandhlophe went on to see a friend and told her he would

join her later. Khathazile attended to some household chores, instructed Mlepheni to spread out the mats on the floor in the dining room and settle the younger children down for the night. She prepared the bed in the same room for the visitors. Bafana informed her that he would not be sleeping at her kraal that night, he would be going to his sister Thandiwe. Khathazile, quite exhausted by then, retired into her bedroom, and promptly fell asleep. She did not hear Bafana leave, but was awakened by Mandhlophe much later that night, or more in the early part of the morning. They went into the kitchen and it was then that they heard dogs barking.

Khathazile went out to look. It was a moonless night. She saw nothing, and the barking had stopped. She walked round the outside of the kitchen, and to her horror stumbled into a policeman; she screamed, then she saw what seemed to her hundreds of policemen, they were all over the place and they were all pointing their guns at her.

One of them was shouting at her. He was a white policeman but he was shouting in Zulu, *'Baphi lababafana kade behlezi lapha?'* (Where are the boys who were here?) She was tongue-tied and cold with fear. Everything went wrong with her body. She lost control of her bowels and her bladder. She was sweating, the questions were coming at her like volcanic eruptions, louder, angrier. She would have rather died than point out the boys. A torch was flashed in her face, a hand grabbed her shoulder, she felt the butt of a gun in her spine. They were pushing her around the kitchen, and to the kitchen door, a policeman at the back of her, another at her side. Yet a third flung a flare into the air which lit up the kraal in a blinding flash. 'Who's there?' she heard one demanding, pointing to the kitchen. Words fell out of her mouth: 'M . . . M . . . Mandhlophe,' 'Who is he?' 'My lover.' 'And who else?' 'My children.' 'And who else?' 'No one.' She heard herself screaming now. 'Damned bitch,' a policeman was swearing, 'damned fucking liar,' and they shouted to Mandhlophe to come out, and he came out, scared and tongue-tied like herself, and they pushed the two of them towards the dining hut and they were shouting at her to open the door and she was pushing the door; and as she did so there was a barrage of shots and she felt the pressure on her spine slacken and the policeman behind her fall. In the same

138

instant there was a blast of fire from the opposite direction and Mandhlophe fell. By now she was running towards Tholakele's kraal screaming, 'I am dying! They are dying – my children! Mhlepheni!'

Mhlepheni was fast asleep on the mat with the other three children. The blaze of light from the flare woke her up. At first she thought it was lightning. The younger children were also startled in their sleep, and ran to her. But when she looked up, she saw Themba and Mpumelelo standing, their guns drawn. She grew afraid, as she had never known fear before, and she moved towards them; the children followed her, but the men indicated to them to hide under the table. They were whispering. The youngest child was about to cry. She put her hand over his mouth and smothered the cry, not quite knowing why she did so, but believing that it was a matter of life and death, and whatever was outside should not hear them. They were all crouching under the table, when something was thrown into the hut and there was a blast. A policeman had crept to the window from the roadside next to their sleeping-huts and had thrown in a hand grenade. It just missed the children. Simultaneously the front door was pushed open and the men began shooting. The shooting went on for quite a while. Then to her horror, Themba pointed his gun at his comrade and he fell dead and she screamed. Themba looked at her for a fleeting moment. She will never forget that look on his face. She had never seen such a look on anyone's face before. It was a look of goodness, as she recalls it now, and then he turned his gun towards himself and in the next split second he was dead.

Mhlepheni was utterly stunned, but she was pulled out of her momentary stupor by her mother's screams. She was calling their names and crying as if they were dead. Mhlepheni grabbed the children; and ran out. She does not know how they made it through that fire, but they made it and rushed towards their mother.

The flare thrown into the air also awakened Tholakele, Salusha's daughter-in-law. Tholakele ran to her window and saw what appeared to her too to be hundreds of policemen. She shook her children awake, grabbed the youngest in her arms and shouted to the others to run, and they were running when they heard the shots and saw Khathazile flinging her arms wildly,

139

shouting for her children and swearing at Bafana; then they saw Khathazile's children bound out of the hut. They almost collided into each other, the two women and their children. Tholakele saw that Khathazile was beyond thinking, so she guided the group to Xhakaza's kraal, a few metres from their own, to leave their children there and go on to Salusha.

The people at Xhakaza's too had been alerted by the shooting and were crouching in consternation in their huts, but Mavis volunteered to go with the two women, and the three of them set off for Salusha's kraal. They saw a light ahead on the road, and drew back. It made them think of the ghost that people said haunted the area. So they changed direction and criss-crossed across the bush, walking through the nettles and black-jacks that stung their feet, stuck to their clothes and slowed down their steps, but they had each other to bolster their spirits and firm their hearts.

The dawn was already breaking when they reached Dayeni and there was the first stirring into the daily routine at Salusha's kraal. Ma Omkhulu was already at the *inqolobe* scratching in the grains to get fowl food. She had not heard the shots, even though sound travels far in the stillness of the country. Younger ears that could have heard had slept through it. The tranquility that bathed the kraal in that early hour, broken only by the bird calls and the cock crows, gently rousing the dreamers into wakefulness, attested to its innocence. Khathazile's uncontrollable screams pierced that tranquility, and exploded it, shattering whatever sleep remained in those 21 huts. Men and women came out in alarm. Salusha was already outside his hut when Khathazile and Tholakele reached him. He succeeded in calming Khathazile down, but he had to rely on Tholakele to make sense of what had happened. As usual his wisdom held him in reasonable calm.

Khathazile kept crying that Bafana had ruined her, that all the police were dead. Bafana stood by stunned. His mother Zanele, fearing for him, tried to console Khathazile but she was inconsolable. She was crying hysterically and shouting, 'My children, my children,' and no sooner than she had come was running back to her kraal. Tholakele followed her, charged by Khathazile to fear for the safety of her own children.

By the time they reached their kraals, the sun had climbed

some considerable paces in the sky and it was broad daylight. They were stopped by police as they neared their kraal. One of them, recognising Khathazile, grabbed her by her shoulders and pushed her towards her hut where the shooting had occurred, and there, as her heart wrenched in agony, she saw Mandhlophe, dead on the ground, and near him, under him, or on top of him, was the policeman who had been talking to her hours earlier. She instinctively gave out a cry of grief, but now there were several policemen, kicking her and boxing her and shouting at her all at once. 'Look what you have done!' one was saying. 'Look what you have done to my police,' another was saying. The police who had accosted her on the road restrained them, and they stopped for a while, but then they began assaulting her again. Then they forced her inside the room and she saw the dead bodies of the young men Bafana had brought, and this time she cried in her heart and cursed Bafana. She was handcuffed, taken away. She could not understand why she had been arrested for the work Bafana had done.

The police then descended on Salusha's kraal and took him in as well.

There was an *impimpi* in their kraal – a terrible *impimpi*. This was clear to everyone. Who was he? The suspicion fell on Bafana. He had been with the men for two days, then on the night of the shoot-out he had conveniently left Khathazile's kraal for Thandiwe's, and when the police came to arrest Salusha, he had disappeared.

Salusha wanted to believe that no son of his would do such a thing, that Kuphelokwakhe must be the *impimpi*.

Whoever the *impimpi*, Bafana, whose handsome young face still bears the traces of his childhood, denied emphatically that he had done so evil a deed. He could not have, he swears. He admired and loved Themba and Mpumelelo too much. He had been surprised when he had bumped into them on Friday. He continues to insist that in taking them to Khathazile's he had merely followed what he believed to have been his father's orders, though they had not come to him directly from his father.

He says he was so frightened when he heard Khathazile blame him that he had run off to Durban to hide in Kwa-Mashu, but pursued by fear and by his conscience at the arrest of his father, he had decided to give himself up to the police. He was on his way to Dayeni on January 17, and waiting for a bus at the Greyville station, when the police had arrested him. He said they were accompanied by a fellow pupil who had pointed him out to them. He was detained and assaulted until his mind was disoriented and he hardly knew what he was saying. He said he passed through periods of unconsciousness and semi-consciousness; that he tried to cling to the facts as he knew them, but eventually he said what he was asked to say, and when he had given evidence to their satisfaction, the police had released him.

The net that the police cast that January did not stop with Salusha, Khathazile and Bafana. Many in the *induna's* district were taken in for questioning; many were released; but Bafana, his mother Zanele, Salusha's older son Michael, his councillor Kuphelokwakhe and Khathazile's common-law husband Hlongwane were detained as state witnesses. Mzamo Zulu, who had been convicted before the trial, was the principal state witness. They had arrested, tried and convicted him for terrorism and brought him down from Robben Island to testify for the state.

Salusha would not have expected, in his wildest dreams, that members of his own family would stand up in court against him. But then he had experienced the terror of the police himself. If he had withstood that terror better, he thought, it was only because he was older and stronger, and the lies they had tried to pour into his ears had not terrified his heart so that he told them the truth when he swore on the Bible. Bafana was only a child, and his mother Zanele was thinking of the safety of her child.

It wasn't what they said in court that put him and Khathazile in the position in which they found themselves. It was the white people's need to extract payment for the white blood that had been spilled. Mzamo was not a bad man. He knew him to be a good man. He told the court that he had not told Salusha everything, that he had kept the true purpose of his mission secret because he knew that Salusha was a straightforward man, and if he had told him all, he, Salusha, would have refused to have anything to do with the matter.

And that was true. He would have done the king's work and he would have done the work of his own church, but if he thought that he was required to do anything that went against his king and his church, he would have refused, and he would have warned his king against the harm that was intended.

Salusha and Khathazile were kept in police custody for over a year before they were finally found guilty and sentenced. The state refused to grant them bail. In that time they learnt of the 'crimes' they had presumably committed and in the process became enlightened about things they had not known before. They learned about Mandela and Biko, about the ANC and the Umkhonto-We-Sizwe, and it only served to increase their admiration for the young Phangode martyrs.

The black police who testified against them swore on the Bible that the two accused had helped terrorists and had intended to overthrow the white government. They said that they had visited Salusha regularly, about once a month, and regularly warned him against *amaphekula*. They had told him that *amaphekula* were dangerous, that they left the country to return and bomb bridges and buildings and recruit young people for the ANC and PAC which were banned organisations, that they brought in guns and explosives and that they killed and destroyed.

Salusha listened in bewilderment. The police did visit him, but not as regularly as they made out, and it seemed to him more to enjoy some beer and enter into flirtatious talk with the women than to educate him about *amaphekula*, a word he heard for the first time after his detention. Even if they had told him what they said they had, it would have made little sense to him, apart from informing him that there were people who did the things they said they did. He would never have seen Themba and Mpumelelo as the powerful people the police were talking about. These were mere boys, good boys, and in the short time they had been in his kraal, everyone had come to love them. There had been such sadness when they had died, and while it was their coming that had brought such calamity into his life, he did not blame them for it. He had seen that one of them had a gun, but there was nothing exceptional about that. Many people had guns in his area. It wasn't easy living in Nongoma. People did not have enough land and they transgressed over each other's boundaries and this led to quarrelling and faction fighting. You could not depend on the police to defend you when you were attacked. You had to defend yourself.

143

The police had also said that he was a member of the ANC, a follower of Mandela. He followed only his king and he followed his church. He followed his king to parliament and to the great rallies in honour of the founder of the Zulu nation, King Shaka. And he followed his bishop, Shembe, for Shembe was sent to them by the powerful kings of the past. Why should he follow the ANC, and why should he follow Mandela? He who knew of Dingaan and Senzangakhona, and who had inherited power through their line. He honoured the ways of his forefathers, he was comfortable in those ways. Why should he want to change all that? Even now he did not understand what the ANC would do, how it would benefit the people. It was as if the government and the ANC were two great kings fighting each other. Kings fought for their own gains. It did not affect the people.

He knew the meaning of justice. He did not sit high as the magistrate did, and he did not make the accused stand as they made him stand. He did not have an expensive building for justice. They sat under the tree and they sat together, he and his councillors and the complainant and the accused, and they talked it out until the right decision was reached and that was justice.

He had told the court, 'I can count with my fingers. I can't sign my name. I do not know dates. I do not know what month is November. . . . I can't say a thing about weeks or months. I do not know how many days in the month. I know how many days there are in a week, and as I plough I know that the sixth day is Sabbath. There are six days in a week.' And indeed in his church there were six days in a week. Salusha had little need to know time beyond the rising and the setting of the sun. Everything happened in his life between these two points and whatever happened happened with a comforting regularity.

But that regularity of events had changed suddenly and shockingly in the first month of January 1985, and since then he had been wrenched from his own cycle of meaning and security and plunged into the nightmarish whirlpool of the white system.

At the end of one year and two months in detention, Salusha was sentenced to five years' imprisonment, Khathazile to three years'. There were pleadings in mitigation and the magistrate showed some mercy. He suspended all of Khathazile's sentence, and two years of Salusha's. His wives waited outside the court as the old grey-haired patriarch was returned again to prison, this time to Robben Island. Omkhulu's wails were the loudest since she had spent the longest years with him. 'He is old,' she said, her eyes grey with age and dim with grief. 'He passed eighty years many years ago. Please take his matter to a higher court and let him come home.'

He serves his sentences where Mandela served most of his, and sends agonising messages to his family when he can. The wheels of justice grind slowly. Is it justice at all? Four months have passed and even now the date of appeal has not been set.

Salusha waits.

Omkhulu waits.

Cemetery unrest: premature resurrection

Dedicated with love to my late father, a Pastor, who buried some of the people whose graves were exhumed to make way for a dam in

had learnt the same respect for these men of SWAPO, even though they were black. He even considered them as comrades.

The doctors at the military hospital in Pretoria had not understood his condition. They did not allow for his sorrow at Lettie's death, and his comradeship with his SWAPO interrogators. They simply thought that he had been brainwashed. Juriaan was given shock treatments, and spent weeks in a ward at the military hospital. It took time before he was able to reclaim his memories. Everything was confused, and the events of his life were like pieces of a jigsaw puzzle. He was still trying to fit the pieces together. The farm was always at the centre, and Lettie was like an angel in the sky, and then there was that dangerous path through the mountains which led to Angola.

Juriaan tethered the horse – Wolraad Woltemade – to a willow tree. The horse was silver in the moonlight, and the river sang sweetly just as it had done in the old days, when he and Lettie were still together.

Tonight he carried an army service revolver, and had a mission. He moved stealthily towards the farmhouse, and looked up at the bedroom window where the capitalist, Johan Grové, lay asleep. He reached the front door, and entered the house with his old key. He even felt like a lover who in the old days, when Lettie was well, would have taken his place beside her in the double bed, and possessed her with a gentle passion. Then he remembered that things were different, and he was a man, who had been ravaged by the war in Angola.

Juriaan pushed open the bedroom door, and was relieved to find that Lettie was not there. It would have been too much for him to have encountered her beauty again. Instead, he stared at the flabby face of Johan Grové. He searched the old man's features for signs of avarice and corruption, but found none. There was much more in the face of Johan Grové than greed. He saw images of other old men there. He even found the face of his father, as well as that of Dominee Frederick van der Merwe, who had tried to teach him the Bible years ago. Then, Johan Grové's eyes opened, but Juriaan did not pull the trigger. He was transfixed by the old man's stare, and the fact that he did not cry out, or speak in anger. Instead, Johan Grové spoke to him in the soft voice of his old schoolteacher, Willem Kemp.

'Juriaan, it's you. But don't you feel that it's a little late to call on me. It must be after midnight. Still, I'm glad that you are here. I often think of you as the war hero of the *platteland*. You are one of South Africa's bravest sons, and the State President gave you a medal. We are all proud of you. . . .'

Juriaan faltered, and remembered that he had never been able to answer Meneer Kemp's questions when he was at school. He had also failed to talk about his doubts about God with Dominee van der Merwe. He recalled the plump hands of the State President, and his fatherly face, when he had bestowed South Africa's highest military honour. Juriaan wept now, not for the death of Lettie, but rather for himself. He had been humiliated in that Angolan town, and suffered an agony, which was like that of Christ, who had carried the cross so long ago in Palestine. His gun was useless, and he even realised that Steven Molefe and Moses Moloi and the other comrades were all lost souls in Africa. The border war was the catalyst in which whites and blacks were thrown together not only in senseless combat but also in a strange kind of dialogue.

Juriaan at last understood the truth, which had eluded him in that ward of the military hospital after he had undergone the shock treatments. He recognised that he was indeed a 'white man', who was ready to defend his country, and took pride in being an Afrikaner. Then a shot rang out, and Juriaan's life ended. Kaptein Pieter Blankenberg stood in the doorway of the bedroom, and held a revolver. Johan Grové sat up in bed, his face ashen with the anguish of the moment.

He whispered, 'You have killed an innocent man. . . .'

'It was my duty to protect you. . . .'

'Juriaan was a late night visitor, not an intruder. . . .'

'He was dangerous, and also a terrorist. . . .'

Kaptein Blankenberg knelt beside Juriaan's body, as if searching for further evidence. Then he stood up, and presented his case to Johan Grové.

'Mr Grové, please understand that Juriaan never recovered from that brainwashing which he received in Angola. It was as if a stranger returned to us, and the real Juriaan died on the battlefield like a hero. The man that returned was no better than a SWAPO terrorist. I had no alternative but to kill him. . . .'

Johan Grové turned away, and his eyes were filled with tears.

The seeds of anarchy were being sown not only in the townships, but also by clever provocateurs like Kaptein Pieter Blankenberg. The night was suddenly chill and clouds obscured the moon. The land out there, which only moments ago had been silver, now lay in the shadow of death.

Ebony statues

THE COMING OF THE CHRIST-CHILD

Bessie Head

He was born on a small mission station in the Eastern Cape and he came from a long line of mission-educated men; great-grandfathers, grandfathers and even his own father had all been priests. Except for a brief period of public activity, the quietude and obscurity of that life was to cling around him all his days. Later, in the turmoil and tumult of his life in Johannesburg, where Christmas Eve was a drunken riot, he liked to tell friends of the way in which his parents had welcomed the coming of the Christ-Child each Christmas Eve:

'We would sit in silence with bowed heads; just silent like that for a half an hour before midnight. I still like the way the old people did it. . . .'

One part of the history of South Africa was also the history of Christianity because it was only the missions that represented a continuous effort to strengthen black people in their struggle to survive, and provided them with a tenuous link between past and future. The psychological battering the older generations underwent was so terrible as to reduce them to a state beyond the non-human. It could also be said that all the people unconsciously chose Christianity to maintain their compactness, their whole-ness and humanity, for they were assaulted on all sides as primitives who were two thousand years behind the white man in civilisation. They were robbed of everything they possessed – their land and cattle – and when they lost everything, they brought to Christianity the same reverence they had once offered to tribe, custom and ancestral worship. The younger generations remembered the elders; Christianity created generations of holy people all over the land.

And so the foundations of a new order of life were laid by the missions, and since the ministry was a tradition in his own

155

family, its evolutionary pattern could be traced right from his great-grandfather's time when the lonely outpost mission church was also the first elementary school existing solely to teach the Bible. From Bible schools, children began to scratch on slates and receive a more general education, until a number of high schools and one university college, attached to missions, spread like a network throughout the land. He was a product of this evolutionary stream and by the time he was born his family enjoyed considerable prestige. They were affluent and lived in a comfortable house, the property of the church, which was surrounded by a large garden. Their life belonged to the community; their home life was the stormy centre of all the tragedies that had fallen on the people, who, no matter which way they turned, were defaulters and criminals in their own land. Much is known about the fearful face of white supremacy, its greed and ruthless horrors. They fell upon the people like a leaden weight and they lay there, an agonising burden to endure.

One day there was – but then there were so many such days – a major catastrophe for the church. The police entered during the hour of worship (it was a point with all the white races of the land that no part of a black man's life was sacred and inviolable) and arrested most of the men as poll tax defaulters. The issue at that time was how people with an income of twenty shillings a year could pay a poll tax of twenty shillings a year. There was only such misery in the rural areas, grandly demarcated as the 'native reserves'. Land was almost non-existent and people thrust back into the reserves struggled to graze stock on small patches of the earth. The stock were worthless, scabby and diseased and almost unsaleable. Starving men with stock losses were driven into working on the mines and the Boer farms for wages just sufficient to cover their poll tax. When their labour was no longer needed in the mines they were endorsed back to the mythical rural areas. There was no such thing as the rural areas left – only hard patterns of greed of which all the people were victims. It was impressed on people that they were guilty of one supposed crime after another and in this way they were conditioned to offer themselves as a huge reservoir of cheap labour.

Thus it was that the grubby day-to-day detail of human misery unfolded before the young man's eyes. Often only five shillings stood between a man and his conviction as a defaulter of some kind, and it was his father's habit to dip deep into his own pocket or the coffers of the church to aid one of his members. That day of the mass arrest of the men in church was to linger vividly in the young man's mind. His father walked up and down for some time, wringing his hands in distress, his composure shaken to the core. Then he had attempted to compose himself and continue the disrupted service, but a cynical male voice in the congregation shouted:

'Answer this question, Father. How is it that when the white man came here, he had only the Bible and we the land. Today, he has the land and we the Bible,' and a second disruption ensued from weeping women whose husbands were among those arrested.

From habit the old man dropped to his knees and buried his face in his hands. The remainder of his congregation filed out slowly with solemn faces. He knelt like that for some time, unaware that his son stood quietly near, observing him with silent, grave eyes. He was a silent, pleasant young man, who often smiled. He liked reading most and could more often than not be found with his head buried in a book. Maybe his father was praying. If so, his son's words cut so sharply into the silence that the old man jerked back his head in surprise.

'There is no God, Father,' the young man said in his quiet way. 'These things are done by men and it is men we should have dealings with. God is powerless to help us, should there even be such a thing.'

'Do you get these ideas from books, my son?' his father asked, uncertainly. 'I have not had the education you are having now because there was no University College in my days, so I have not travelled as far as you in loss of faith, even though I live in the trough of despair.'

This difference in views hardly disrupted the harmonious relationship between father and son. Later, people were to revere an indefinable quality in the young politician, not realising that he rose from the deep heart of the country, where in spite of all that was said, people were not the 'humiliated, downtrodden blacks', but men like his father. Later, he was to display a courage, unequalled by any black man in the land. The romance and legends of the earlier history still quivered in the air of the rural area where he was born. Nine land wars had the tribes fought against the British. Great kings like Hintsa had conducted the wars, and in spite of the grubbiness and despair of the present, the older generations still liked to dwell on the details of his death. Hintsa had been a phenomenon, a ruler so brilliant that on his death his brains had been removed from his head so that some part of him could remain above ground to be revered and worshipped. It was a tradition of courage that his people treasured.

On graduating from university he did not choose the ministry as his career. Instead, he had one of those rare and elegant positions as Professor of Bantu Languages at the University of the Witwatersrand in Johannesburg. He was as elegant and cultured as his job and ahead of him stretched years and years of comfort and security. The black townships surrounding the city of Johannesburg absorbed genius of all kinds in astounding combinations. The poor and humble and the rich and talented lived side by side. Brilliant black men, with no outlet for their talents for management and organisation, were the managers and organisers of huge crime rings around the country with vast amounts of men in their employ. They flashed about the townships in flashy American cars of the latest design and sold their stolen goods at backdoor prices to the millions of poor, honest black labourers who served the city. Johannesburg was the pulsing heart of the land; everything of significance that happened in the country first happened in Johannesburg. It was also the centre of the big labour shuttle; the gold mines stretching along the Witwatersrand, with their inexhaustible resources, needed thousands and thousands of black hands to haul those riches above ground. The city was complex, as international as the gold that flowed to all the banking houses of the world. It had also been the centre of ruthless exploitation and major political protest, and it seemed to have aged in cynicism and weariness ahead of the rest of the country. It was a war-weary and apathetic world that he entered in 1948. It was as though people said: 'Ah, political protest? You name it, we've done it. What is it all for?' It took something new and fresh to stir the people out of their apathy and exhaustion.

Almost immediately he attracted a wide range of thinking men. Immediately, the details of his life attracted interest and he slipped into the general colour of the environment. But he carried almost the totality of the country with him. It wasn't so much his reading habits – there were hundreds of men there acquainted with Karl Marx and the Chinese revolution; there were hundreds of men there who wore their intellectual brilliance as casually as they wore their clothes. It was the fillers he provided on parts of the country that were now myths in the minds of urban dwellers – the strange and desperate struggles waged by people in the rural areas.

'I've just been reading this book on some of the land struggles in China after the revolution,' he'd say. 'It was difficult for Mao Tse-Tung to get people to cultivate land because ancestor worship was practised there. I've seen people do the same thing in the Transkei where I was born. There was hardly any land left to cultivate but people would rather die of starvation than plough on the land where their ancestors were buried. . . .'

Almost nightly there was an eager traffic of friends through his home. He enjoyed the circle of friends that gathered round him. He enjoyed knocking out his ideas against the ideas of other men and it was almost as though he were talking an unintelligible language. His friends no longer knew of the sacred values of the tribes – that all people had ever once wanted was a field where they may plough their crops and a settled home near the bones of their ancestors. Like the young men of his circle, he was a member of the Youth League of an organisation that for forty-seven years had been solely representative of the interests of black people. They had brought people out on the streets on protests and demonstrations. People had been shot dead and imprisoned. A strange hypnotic dialogue pervaded the country. It was always subtly implied that black people were violent; yet it had become illegal in the year 1883 for black men to possess arms. They had little beyond sticks and stones with which to defend themselves. Violence was never a term applied to white men, but they had arms. Before these arms the people were cannon fodder. Who was violent?

Year after year, at convention after convention, this kindly body of the people's representatives mouthed noble sentiments.

'Gentlemen, we ought to remember that our struggle is a non-violent one. Nothing will be gained by violence. It will only harden the hearts of our oppressors against us. . . .'

In 1957 there were more dead black bodies to count. Gopane village, eighteen miles outside the small town of Zeerust in the Transvaal, was up until that year a quiet and insignificant African village. A way of life had built up over the years – the older people clung to the traditional ways of ploughing their fields and sent their children to Johannesburg, either to work or to acquire an education. In 1957 a law was passed compelling black women to carry a 'pass book'. Forty years ago the same law had been successfully resisted by the women who had offered themselves for imprisonment rather than carry the document. The 'pass book' had long been in existence for black men and was the source of excruciating suffering. If a man walked out of his home without his 'pass book' he simply disappeared from society for a stretch of six months or so. Most men knew the story. They supplied a Boer farmer for six months with free labour to harvest his potatoes. A 'boss-boy' stood over the 'prisoners' with a whip. They dug out potatoes with such speed that the nails on their fingers were worn to the bone. The women were later to tell a similar tale but in that year, 1957, people still thought they could protest about laws imposed on them. Obscure Gopane village was the first area in the country where the 'pass book' was issued to women. The women quietly accepted them, walked home, piled them in a huge heap and burnt them. Very soon the village was surrounded by the South African police. They shot the women dead. From then onwards 'pass books' were issued to all black women throughout the country without resistance.

Was it sheer terror at being faced with nameless horrors who would shoot unarmed women dead or did the leaders of the people imagine they represented a respectable status quo? There they were at the very next convention, droning on again:

'Gentlemen,' said speaker number one, an elderly, staid, complacent member of the community. 'Gentlemen, in spite of the tragedy of the past year, we must not forget that our struggle is essentially a non-violent one. . . .'

He was going on like that – after all the incident had passed into history and let's attend to matters at hand – when there was a sudden interruption of the sort that had not disrupted those decorous, boring proceedings for years. Someone had stood up out of turn. Speaker number one looked down his nose in disdain. It was the young Professor of Bantu Languages. He was only in the Youth League section and of no significance.

'Gentlemen!' And to everyone's amazement the young man's voice quivered with rage. 'May I interrupt the speaker! I am heartily sick of the proceedings of this organisation. Our women were recently killed in a violent way and the speaker still requests of us that we follow a non-violent policy. . . .'

'What are you suggesting that we do?' asked speaker number one, alarmed. 'Are you suggesting that we resort to violence against our oppressors?'

'I wish that the truth be told!' And the younger man banged his hand on the table in exasperation. 'Our forefathers lived on this land long before the white man came here and forced a policy of dispossession on us. We are hardly human to them! They only view us as objects of cheap labour! Why is the word *violence* such a terrible taboo from *our* side! Why can't we state in turn that *they* mean nothing to us and that it is our intention to get them off our backs! How long is this going to go on? It will go on and on until we say: NO MORE!' And he flung his arms wide in a gesture of desperation. 'Gentlemen! I am sick of the equivocation and clever talk of this organisation. If anyone agrees with me, would they please follow me,' and he turned forthwith and left the convention hall.

Everything had happened so abruptly that there was a moment's pause of startled surprise. Then half the assembly stood up and walked out after the young man, and so began a new short era in the history of political struggle in South Africa. His political career lasted barely a year. George Padmore's book *Pan Africanism or Communism* was the rage in Johannesburg at that time and he and his splinter group allied themselves with its sentiments.

In spite of the tragedies of the country, that year seemed to provide a humorous interlude to the leaders of the traditional people's movement. Their whole attention was distracted into ridiculing the efforts of their new rival; they failed to recognise a creative mind in their midst. The papers that were issued in a steady stream were the work of a creative artist and not that of a hardened self-seeking politician. The problems they outlined were always new and unexpected. They began slowly from the bottom, outlining basic problems:

'We can make little progress if our people regard themselves as inferior. For three hundred years the whites have inculcated a feeling of inferiority in us. They only address us as "boy" and "girl", yet we are men and women with children of our own and homes of our own. Our people would resent it if we called them "kwedini" or "mfana" or "moshemane", all of which means "boy". Why then do they accept indignity, insult and humiliation from the white foreigner. . . ?'

A counter paper was immediately issued by the people's traditional movement:

'We have some upstarts in our midst who have promised to lead the people to a new dawn but they are only soft gentlemen who want to be "Sir-ed" and "Madam-ed". Who has led the people in mass demonstrations? Who is the true voice of the people . . . ?'

They arranged for stones to be cast at him as he addressed public rallies and for general heckling and disruption of the proceedings. Yet during that single year he provided people with a wide range of political education such as the traditional people's movement had not been able to offer in all their long history. His papers touched on everything from foreign investment in the land which further secured the bonds of oppression to some problems of the future which were phrased as questions:

'Can we make a planned economy work within the framework of a political democracy? It has not done so in any of the countries that practise it today. . . . We cannot guarantee minority rights because we are fighting precisely that group-exclusiveness which those who plead for minority rights would like to perpetuate. Surely we have guaranteed the highest if we have guaranteed individual liberties . . . ?'

The land could be peaceful for months, even years. There was a machinery at hand to crush the slightest protest. Men either fled its ravenous, insensitive brutal jaws, or, obsessed as a few men often are with making some final noble gesture or statement, they walked directly into the brutal jaws. It was always a fatal decision. No human nobility lit up the land. People were hungry for ideas, for a new direction, yet men of higher motivation were irresistibly drawn towards the machine. That machine was already gory with human blood and since it was only a machine it remained unmoved, unshaken, unbroken. Obsessed with clarifying a legality, he walked directly into the machine. The laws of the land were all illegal, he said. They were made exclusively by a white minority without consulting the black majority. It was a government of a white minority for a white minority; therefore the black majority was under no moral obligation to obey its laws. At his bidding thousands of black men throughout the land laid down their 'pass books' outside the gates of the police stations.

He had a curious trial. White security police had attended all his public meetings and taken notes but there were no witnesses for the State except one illiterate black policeman. He gave a short halting statement that made people in the public gallery roar with laughter.

'I attended a political gathering addressed by this man. I heard him say: The pass book. That is our water-pipe to parliament.'

There were sixty-nine dead bodies outside a Sharpeville police station. He was sentenced to three years' imprisonment for sedition. Then a special bill was passed to detain him in prison for life. He was released after nine years, but served with so many banning orders that he could barely communicate with his fellow men. Then he became ill and died.

An equivalent blanket of silence fell upon the land. The crackdown on all political opposition was so severe that hundreds quailed and fled before the monstrous machine. It was the end of the long legend of non-violent protest. But a miracle people had not expected was that from 1957 onwards the white man was being systematically expelled from Africa, as a political force, as a governing power. Only the southern lands lay in bondage. Since people had been silenced on such a massive scale, the course and direction of events was no longer theirs. It had slipped from their grasp some time ago into the hands of the men who were training for revolution.

When all was said and done and revolutions had been fought and won, perhaps only dreamers longed for a voice like the man who was as beautiful as the coming of the Christ-Child.

163

NO SHELTER
FOR CLEANERS

Miriam Tlali

Mrs T H, you have come to speak to me about the conditions under which you work as an office-cleaner in Johannesburg.

Yes. First, I was working in Nedbank in Wolmarans Street in the city. I suffered because on my way from work I was the only one on *this* side – that is, in White City. All the others I used to work with were living in the other townships like Klipspruit, Orlando, Mofolo; they went only as far as Crossroads. *This* side, in the 'Number One' Office area, I was the only one. I had to alight at that corner alone every morning very early. We used to get off the train at Nancefield station and take the first bus home. Three times I nearly got injured at that Number One Office corner. Then I realised that, no – I shall soon sustain serious injuries. So I decided to sleep at the Johannesburg Park Station. But even there, too, they chase us away and they don't want us. Even if you have your monthly train ticket with you, they don't *want* you. They only want those with Main Line tickets. So in dark nights, pouring rain and freezing cold weather they chase you away. . . . Do you see where the rickshaws used to line up, just outside the station? (*I nodded.*) That's where I used to perch myself just so that dawn may come and that I may get into the train. The whole of 1972 I used to sleep there in the street, waiting for the night to pass. Because even in the trains (there used to be a Naledi train which stopped on the platform) the police used to come and chase us out of it, right there from inside it. We used to wonder and ask ourselves. . . . Just what *is* there for us to do? Then in 1973, in May, I was transferred to R. There, too, the cleaners used to be ordered out. Then one day one of the white men there saw me early in the morning. Then he asked the 'boss-boy' whether the cleaners are allowed to sleep at the premises, and the 'boss-boy' said: 'I don't know because

164

when I arrive in the morning, they are not there.' Then the 'boss-boy' approached us and told us. I then said to the 'boss-boy': 'Tell the white man that it is true that we sleep here because we are afraid of the hooligans, we only seek temporary shelter. We knock off early and we wait until it is safe.' Anyway, they allowed us to spend the time before dawn there.

Whereabouts did you sleep – at what part of the premises?

In the garage. On the cement floors next to the cars. We did not mind as long as it was 'a safe place'. We are thankful. We used to take cardboard boxes, spread them on the floor and lie down. But as soon as it was five o'clock, we were to be *out*. All this time we were working like that. Now we are out of there. We have changed to Ranleigh House.

Who changed you, the white people?

No. Our contract there ended and we had to leave. We went somewhere else. We are at Ranleigh House. But with them, too, it's the same old story. When we knock off at 2.30 a.m., we have to go. All of us, at that time, we have to go. There's no mercy. Even if it's two o'clock we have to go. Now it is many people, in many places who have been assaulted, people who work at night, meeting the 'ducktails' and 'tsotsis' – many, many people. I don't know about Ranleigh House because we've only just started there. But in all the other places, we have been hearing of many of God's people who have been injured. Others we see passing near where we work on their way out, going to . . . we don't know where. Now, one asks oneself, just what happens to these people? . . . We are not to go to Park Station; we may not sleep on the benches, we may not sit in the waiting-rooms. We must stand outside. Even when there's a train on the platform, we may not board it. Now we wonder where we must go to because in the locations at that time it is 'rough' (*unsafe*). Even then too, where will you go to at that time because most likely you are the only one in that neighbourhood where you stay? It is like that too in Ranleigh House.

At 2 a.m. what happens – do they come and sign you off?

Yes. Someone gives us the order to leave. We have a white woman, a supervisor. When we go, she comes and lets us off.

Now the cleaners – is it only women that they employ?

Yes. It's only women who are cleaners. Some come from Diepkloof, others Naledi, everywhere. She (the supervisor) is also a woman. But she has a car, you see.

They are companies of cleaners. Many firms. These have different names. One is called National, another is B C S and so on. You work until that certain time. It matters not whether it's raining or icy cold, there's no shelter for us.

It is they who must provide shelter, isn't it?

Yes. . . . How we get home, they are not bothered. That is none of their concern. *You* must see what to do. Whether you are assaulted or not, is none of their business. At one time, I've forgotten what year it was, a cousin of mine was working at this Braamfontein 'thing'. (*She raised her arms and pointed upwards with her palms clasped together.*)

Which thing? The Tower (Hertzog Tower)?

Yes. The tower. She was just leaving that place early when she was molested. It was only after they learnt that she was seriously ill and in hospital with bad wounds that the white there said: 'All right, you cleaners can wait in the premises until it is safe to go home.' Those are the difficulties under which we work during the night.

Now this cleaning you do. When do you do it – during their absence?

Yes. We clean after the office-workers have left. Only the 'securities' are present (*the security guards*).

I thought it was the black male workers who do the cleaning.

No. It's *we* the women who do it.

When do you start?

Six.

How do you do it; do you use machines?

Yes. We use the 'Hoovers'.

Now, what happened at one time when you alighted from the bus?

At one time when I got off from the bus I met 'tsotsis'. It was my usual practice to run very fast, as fast as I *could* in the direction where I live. On this occasion, by the time they caught up with me, I was already near my house. The bus driver used to do. . . . He used not to stop at the official bus stop but instead, he used to drop me at the corner of the street where I live. But now they must have noticed that, at *that* particular time, I shall alight. Then they would hide and wait at the house near the corner. One of them tried to reach for me and pull me towards

166

them. Fortunately at that time, I had armed myself with . . . you know, these spiked iron flower holders . . . (*I nodded*) . . . Yes, the steel ones. I had one of those, and I implanted it into his forearm (*she indicated the spot on her own arm*). . . . And when he withdrew and yelled 'inchu-u-u!' I got the chance to run for safety. Then I realised that in spite of the thought that I am clever, I'll get hurt seriously. It was after that incident that I decided to stay at Park Station. . . . Outside. Then I used to take the first train from Faraday to Naledi and stay inside it. It would travel up and down, to and fro like that with me until it was safe to get off at Nancefield and go home. (*We both laughed softly and shook our heads.*)

We are laughing, but this matter is not amusing at all. It's very sad indeed.

Yes, but what can we do? Then you'd hear passengers say to me: 'You'll get hurt in the trains here; going up and down alone, and a woman for that matter.' They were male passengers as usual at that time. Then I would answer: 'What can I do? I've got to try and save my life as I work. I have to work; I have no husband.'

What about children? Haven't you got a son to fetch you from the bus stop? But then, he, too, could easily oversleep and not fetch you.

No; not that. He too can be assaulted while coming to fetch me. . . . For instance, there's another man. His name is Ngubeni. We attend the same church with him. He stays in Mofolo Village. His daughter works for a bakery. She goes to work late at night and knocks off at night. This poor man made it a point to take her to Ikwezi Station. Every night at 8.30 p.m. he fetches her from the station. One night, two months back, after he had taken her to the station . . . you know it was very dark as it was winter. . . . On his way back, he met the 'boys'. They were eight. What did they do to him? If it were not for the fact that God gave him power . . . then I don't know. With the stick he was carrying, he summoned all courage and fought like mad. He fought for his life; for 'final'! When these boys realised that this old man had beaten them, one of them tripped him. That was when they got the chance to over-power him. They tripped him and dropped him on the ground on his back like that. One of them produced a knife and tried to stab him, but he had seen him already and he grabbed the knife. They then clubbed his head and he sustained serious head injuries. It all happened because he tried to save his daughter's life. There are many more people who have been stabbed or killed because they have to come from work too early or too late at night.

Obviously this kind of work has many risks. How much money are you paid; is it much?

No. B C S only pays us R34.

Per week?

No, every two weeks. We are holding on because.... What shall we do? We have children and grandchildren. We have to send them to school. How are we to feed them? There's not much we can do with that R34. We complain but it does not help. How much have we been 'crying' (*appealing*)? . . . It's long but . . . (*She shrugs her shoulders*) . . . How do we pay rent. . . . The money only pays the rent and for a few bags of coal. We just go on. There's nothing we can do with it.

It's good you spoke about this.

It's no good keeping quiet. I've realised it. It's these people who speak lies, telling strangers to Soweto that we live very happily; we eat and drink, and there is nothing we lack. *They* are the ones who are sell-outs. They tell the whites all sorts of untruths about our lives here. . . . You can see. Here in White City Jabavu, they paint the outside walls of the houses; the houses along the main roads so that when the very 'big' ones come, they can deceive them and say: 'Can you see that? We are painting the houses for them. You can see that there's nothing they want that they don't get.' They only clean those houses along the roads instead of letting them come right inside into the passages and so on and see the filth all around.

You know, I never think of this matter of office-cleaning. At first it used to be men who were doing the work, wasn't it? I was aware of female nurses having to do night duty, but not cleaners. What has happened to the men who used to do it?

You know, the men and women who do the cleaning of the flats and so on do the work during the day-time. It is the offices which have to be cleaned at night because during the day, they are being used.

I see, What about your train and bus fares; do they pay for those?

No. We have to pay it from the R34 per fortnight that we get. . . . It's the train and bus fares and also the meals we eat.

Mind you, even Carlton Centre, big as it is, the people who clean it also have to go out of there at that awkward time. . . . In the night, at two o'clock. They have no shelter for the cleaners.

Just reckon how far Ranleigh House is from the station. . . . At times we move from there and come across 'ducktails', white men looking for black prostitutes. They mistake us for street-walkers. They too are an additional menace. They drive along the streets next to the pavements, following us and making advances; enticing us to go into their cars. You never know what the real intention is. As soon as one disappears round the corner, another one appears.

INTERVIEW WITH MRS ALBERTINA SISULU

Miriam Tlali

Mrs Sisulu, you are one of the leading women in our community who are actively engaged in a number of organisations through which women strive for better conditions now and in the future. The Federation of South African Women is one these. Will you please elaborate and mention any of the others.

Before the time of my banning, we had the Federation of South African Women and in addition, we had mothers' organisations which were operating in the townships, helping the needy families. We had a small society which had many branches and which catered especially for those families where the fathers or mothers were gaoled for various so-called 'offences'. These bodies went on even up to 1976. So, apart from the Federation I was in these societies which were formed by women to help other women.

I see. Where exactly did you come from before Soweto? Were you from such places as Sophiatown, George Goch, Western Native Township, Eastern Native Township or what?

I was from the Transkei.

Now, during the time of the removal of Sophiatown where were you?

I was right here.

Mrs Sisulu, you have been engaged in the struggle for change of the prevailing conditions for the Africans — especially for the black women. Your opinion therefore would be very significant and valuable. What do you think. . . . Do you think much has been achieved by way of advancement or the improvement of the lot of black women in particular? Do you think any change for the better has been accomplished socially, economically or politically?

Socially and economically I should think so, because in the olden days, people used to think (and indeed accept) that the place of a woman is in the kitchen. But today they are in leading positions and are holding offices in many spheres. I think that even financially their earnings have improved.

I see. In what capacity are you employed? What is your occupation?

I am a Nursing Sister under the City Health Department.

Where were you qualified?

At the Non-European Hospital, as far back as 1943, the one popularly known as the General Hospital. That was for my General Nursing. For my Midwifery, I was trained at the Bridgman Hospital.

I suppose that was before you met u-Tata-Sisulu?[1]

In fact, I met u-Tata-Sisulu during my training at the Non-European Hospital. We met, got married in 1944, and lived here in Johannesburg all this time.

You were born Miss who?

Thethiwe. Miss Thethiwe.

Coming to your life with u-Tata-Sisulu. . . . Most of your political life revolves around him and the fact that he was involved in the struggle for our liberation, and the consequences of his being a leader of the black people. You undeniably have immense fortitude. For most of your married life, you were faced with an abnormal existence of a wife and mother who has to fend alone without her partner. What exactly makes you strong enough to pull through all this? Where do you draw your inspiration from?

Fortunately for me (without sounding too arrogant or boastful) I married a very clever and brilliant man, I must say. In fact, when

[1]U-Tata
Ntate } : Father (term of respect)

the ANC Youth League was formed, I was the only lady. He used to take me to these meetings and he used to clarify to me whatever I could not understand.

So he never kept you out of his political life at all?

No. I was always fully involved. He kept me informed. Even when I could not attend sometimes, he came back and reported to me all developments, with the result that I also became part and parcel of the political life he led.

I do understand that your husband instilled and cultivated in you the burning desire for total involvement. But I am still not satisfied. Surely there must have been fertile soil on which he planted that seed? There must have been deep down within you the capacity to stand erect, alone and undaunted, to bring up your children, educate them, and most important of all, lead them along the right track to be the responsible people in the community as they are. Can you perhaps say what it is that makes you so strong inwardly?

I think what made me pull through is the fact that I grew up as an orphan and I struggled to get my education. It was therefore always my desire to try and help anybody who was in that unfortunate situation. I also had my younger brothers and sisters to care for. For instance, when I was doing my Standard Four, my mother had a baby and she died shortly after that. Because I was the eldest, I had to leave school and look after the baby. That meant that I had to lose a whole year. Even then, I still had to see to my brothers and sisters, and even educate them. In addition, I felt strongly about our plight as the oppressed *because* when I met my husband he used to explain some of the intricate problems with which we are faced. I combined these unfortunate circumstances, compared them with my own life situation and felt that really, I had no right to be thinking of anything else but to play my humble part in the liberation of my people. I resolved to help whoever was in need.

And your father, when did he pass away?

My father also passed away when we were still very young. I think I am the only one who knew him, that is, of all his children. I used to assist my mother, who was doing all the farming those days.

Now, about your own family. . . . How many children have you got?

I have got five . . . three boys and two girls. At the time of the arrest of u-Tata-Sisulu, the youngest was about six years old. So they were all still young and of schoolgoing age. My baby was attending a crèche.

And you managed?

I managed, all the same. I had to. . . . You know what it is. When the salary comes, it has to cover a lot of items and it was always providing for the urgent needs to survive. It was not easy. At times it was a matter of robbing Peter to pay Paul.

Tell me. . . . How did you feel when Ntate Sisulu was sentenced to life imprisonment?

As my partner, it was very painful. But all the same, I was not caught unawares; I knew what was going to happen. He used to tell me that he doesn't belong to the family and that he would be sent to Robben Island. As early as only a few years after we were married, he used to tell me that his time with us was going to be very short, and that his destiny was that of a man determined to strive for the liberation of his people. He prepared me for what was to come.

And yet immediately after that you set yourself to the task of helping others?

Yes. We started forming the committees I was telling you about. For instance, when Lilian Ngoyi was arrested, we rallied round and assisted her family. We used to collect monies and buy coal, wood, groceries and other items which they needed.

You used to work with Lilian Ngoyi and such people as Mrs Mbele?

Yes, I used to work with both of them. Lilian was one of our great heroines. As for Mrs Mbele, I think of all of us, she is the one who suffered most. I also worked with her. She bore her hardships with great courage. She had three children; one girl and two boys. The boys left the country. In 1975, the eldest son met a car accident in Zambia and he died. Mrs Mbele and I were in and out of gaol together. She used to leave her children with neighbours, what could she do? She had no one. Her husband had died when her children were still very very young. She was dedicated and suffered up to her last days.

You were all actively engaged in the great march to Pretoria?

Yes, we marched to Pretoria. And we were involved in the Defiance Campaign here in Market Street. I was there when we were escorted to Number 4 by the police. Fortunately for me, my mother-in-law was still alive, and she used to remain with the children. For instance, the baby was only ten months and I breast-fed her for the last time the morning I left for gaol.

And yet all those arrests and detentions did not deter you from going on with the struggle?

No. In fact they made me even more determined; they made me more aggressive. Really. Because I resent all the brutality and cruelty which is being exercised against the people.

Mrs Sisulu, there seems to be so much confusion and indecision as far as the education in Soweto is concerned. The Matriculation results, for instance, and the re-examination of students and all that is very depressing and causes anxiety to many parents, teachers and thousands who are interested in our future and the welfare of our children in general. What do you think the solution to all this is, and to all these bottlenecks which keep interrupting the education of our children?

I think the solution is with us. There *is* a solution. The solution lies with the parent and the child. Once we come together and say, 'We don't want this Bantu Education,' it will come to an end. Do you know that in 1955 or so, when Bantu Education was first introduced, we withdrew our children from the schools and they were closed? We set up our own private schools. This very house where we are sitting in now was one of the 'schools'. Those children who could not be accommodated in them, we provided play-centres for. We employed our own teachers and went on giving our children the right type of education.

Unfortunately for us, the government would not register the schools, and we failed. But if we had continued in spite of it all, we would have succeeded. This whole confusion is as a result of deliberate efforts by the government to frustrate and confuse our children. What is worse now is that a girl of eighteen (a boy could perhaps go and work) if she fails Form III, she must leave school and go and do adult education. What's that? Why should such a child be thrust out of school when she is still only a child? That's why I stood up and said at a meeting on Sunday that we want all organisations to be involved, informed and consulted so that, working as a united force, they can make resolutions and execute them together. We have many women's organisations. There are DWEPO, the Federation of South African Women — which deals with all problems affecting the homes. There are the YWCA, COSAS, Housewives' League, all sorts of women's bodies. These, and all bodies in general, could come together and make a strong pressure group against all these discriminatory measures.

You feel that this is a national issue?

This is a national issue, yes. We have to think of it countrywide or as a Province. We should refrain from taking such resolutions as the one which was taken at the meeting on Sunday that all children should boycott examinations on the very following Tuesday. Such decisions can only lead to confusion, because by then, only a handful will be informed of the move and that will lead to failure. Unity is strength. That is what we have been fighting for, after all.

How long were you banned?

Seventeen years.

Do you think these bannings serve any purpose?

No. They do not serve any purpose.

It is now seventeen years[2] since Ntate Sisulu and others were sent to Robben Island. It is the ardent wish of all Africans that

---

[2]This interview took place in 1979. Mr Walter Sisulu is still in prison, now twenty-four years.

he and the other political prisoners be released. In fact, millions in Africa and throughout the world demand for their freedom. What do you feel, do you feel that we should just sit and hope that they will one day be freed, or should we continue to call for their immediate release?

We shall never stop demanding that they be freed. In fact, as far as I am concerned, the day when they will cast away the shackles is not far.

I gather you have been to see him recently. How is his spirit, his disposition?

First-class! He is as strong, as lively and as brave as ever.

Why do you think the banning orders on you have not been renewed? Do you think the government is becoming more lenient, more considerate?

I think the banning orders have not been renewed, *not* because the government's attitude has changed. I think they are just being clever. The whole apparent lull is to me just some kind of window-dressing. After all they have made a lot of noise that they are going to change, whereas there is no such thing. They are only trying to show the world that 'there it is, we have relaxed some of the banning orders', but meanwhile I know that they are watching me. You won't believe me when I say that they are always around watching me. A police van often comes and stops just near my house and it stays there for hours. And that doesn't just take place once in a while. They do that all the time, right through the week sometimes.

What about your son Zwelake, you say you are living with his wife and their two-year-old son. He has now been gaoled for quite a long time hasn't he?

Yes.

In other words detentions and arrests have become a tradition with the Sisulus. Your daughter-in-law is now in the same plight as yourself. This whole harassment is going from one generation to another isn't it?

Yes it is. That is why after I was re-banned, when the reporters asked my children: 'How do you feel?', they replied: 'We are used to this life; this harassment. We grew up under these conditions. They have become part and parcel of our lives. After all, even if our mother is not banned, the police are going to go up and down this house.' You won't believe me when I say that they come at an unholy hour of one o'clock and when you ask them: 'What is it this time?', they say: 'No. We are just doing a general check-up.' Can you believe that? Just to terrorise people. The way they terrorise banned people is really unbelievable. And then they call other people terrorists when *they* are the terrorists. They come at any time and ask you unnecessary questions.

Your banning orders didn't stop you from working?

They tried to, but fortunately for us, we have lawyers and the lawyers warned them not to. After the Anti-Pass Campaign, when I was detained in 1963 (with my first-born son, who was a seventeen-year-old then) I had been gaoled for three whole months under the notorious ninety-day detention – detention without trial. I had not been paid for all that time and, mind you, I was then the sole breadwinner. After that I was suspended from work for two weeks. I suppose there was a tussle over my fate. Then I was reinstated on the third week. At that time, my husband was in hiding. It was during the time of Rivonia. Then I was house-arrested. The first five years of banning were the usual ones – you know, restricting me to the magisterial area of Johannesburg, forbidding me from attending meetings and so on. But the ten years that followed those were the most difficult years of my life. It meant that I must be indoors from 6 p.m. to 6 a.m. the following day and that I must report at the police station every Wednesday of the week, whether it was raining or snowing. You can imagine. . . . You are a mother. You must work, come back and cook, then rush to the police station and be back before 6 o'clock. It was torture! I was not allowed a single visitor. For instance, Mandela's son came here one day to visit my children. Because of that, we had to go up and down to the police station to explain why he had come here. I was accused of having had a visitor and having had supper with him. It was ridiculous because I was banned and not my children, and he had come to *them* and not to me. And they lost that case. Nothing had happened to make them impose such stringent measures. Yet I had made up my mind that I would cope in spite of it all. I wanted to show them that even if they thought that because I'm only a woman, I would not succeed, I would do it. I was not going to play into their hands because I *hate* them. I never broke any of their ridiculous conditions.

Can you go out of this country to see your exiled daughter?

No, I cannot. They cannot give me a passport unless I decide to take a Transkeian passport; and I shall never do that.

Why? Do you not recognise the Homelands?

No I do not. They are just a farce, created to split the people and to delay the struggle. To me, the whole of South Africa is one unit and nothing else.

Finally . . . do these bannings never make you feel cut-off from society?

I am a nurse by profession. I am always with the people. I speak to the people and they speak to me.

Women: more than just a man's spare rib

ABOUT THE
CONTRIBUTORS

■ **Bongiwe Dhlomo** was born in 1956, the daughter of a clergyman. Her talent was quite unrecognised at school, but in 1977, bored and frustrated by secretarial work, she applied to study for the Diploma in Fine Art at the Rorke's Drift Art and Craft Centre, Zululand, and was immediately accepted. She has exhibited her work in South Africa, Botswana and Swaziland, and pictures have been bought by the universities of Natal, Zululand and the Witwatersrand, and by the Durban Art Gallery and the Botswana National Art Gallery. In addition to her series on *Women's roles in South Africa*, reproduced in this book, she has also completed a series called *Removals* (bought by the Durban Art Gallery) and a series called *African Songs*. Bongiwe Dhlomo is at present Project Co-ordinator for the Alexandra Art Centre, Alexandra Township, Johannesburg. She is married to an artist, Kagiso Mautloa and they have two children.

■ **Menán du Plessis**, 33, from Cape Town, has published poetry, literary criticism and a novel, *A State of Fear* (which won the Olive Schreiner Prize in 1984 and the Sanlam Literary Prize in 1986). 'Longlive!' is an extract from her new novel. A member of the United Democratic Front, she works on publications for the organisation, while earning a living by teaching Linguistics at the University of Cape Town.

■ **Sheila Fugard** was born in Birmingham, England, in 1932. Her family moved to South Africa when she was 8. She studied Drama at the University of Cape Town, and in 1956 she married the playwright Athol Fugard; they have one daughter. Her novels include *The Castaways* (1972) which won the CNA Literary Award and the Olive Schreiner Prize, *Rite of Passage* (1976), and *A Revolutionary Woman* (1984). She has had two poetry collections published, *Threshold* (1975) and *Mythic*

Things (1981). She has just completed a new novel, *Faces of the Ancestors*. She lives near Port Elizabeth in the Eastern Cape.

■ **Nadine Gordimer** was born and lives in South Africa. She has written eight novels, including *A Guest of Honour*, which won the James Tait Black Prize, *The Conservationist*, which was co-winner of the Booker Prize in the United Kingdom, *Burger's Daughter*, and most recently *July's People*. Her short stories have been collected in eight volumes. Ms Gordimer has also received the French international literary prize the Grand Aigle d'Or. Her writings have appeared in many American magazines, including *The New Yorker, Harper's, Atlantic Monthly*, and *The New York Review of Books*.

■ **Bessie Head** has been described as 'one of the greatest novelists who ever lived on the continent of Africa'. Born in South Africa, her mother the daughter of a wealthy Natal racing family, her father a black stable hand, she grew up in an orphanage. Later she worked as a teacher and journalist. By 1963 she could no longer endure living under South African racist laws, and settled with her son in Serowe, Botswana. There she wrote *When the Rain Clouds Gather* (1968), *Maru* (1971), *A Question of Power* (1974), a collection of short stories *The Collector of Treasures* (1977), and her tribute to her neighbours, *Serowe, Village of the Rain Wind* (1981). Her death in 1986 at the age of 49 has come as a shock to all those who admired her work and her great talent.

■ **Elsa Joubert** was born in the Cape and educated at Stellenbosch and Cape Town Universities. Subsequently she travelled extensively through Africa and wrote six travel books. Her novels include *To Die at Sunset* and *The Long Journey of Poppie Nongena (Poppie)* which has been translated into ten languages, adapted for the stage and performed in New York, Edinburgh, London, Australia and Canada. She has published short stories in various anthologies in Afrikaans, English and French. She is a Fellow of the Royal Literature Society, and was awarded the Winifred Holtby Prize for *Poppie*. She is married to Klaas Steytler, and has three grown-up children.

■ **Ellen Kuzwayo** has been a 'disgruntled schoolteacher', a social worker, mother, wife, and in her sixties returned to study at the University of the Witwatersrand for a higher qualification in social work. She is president of the Black Consumer Union of South Africa, and of the Maggie Maguba Trust. She was chosen Woman of the Year in 1979 by the Johannesburg newspaper *The Star*, and was nominated again in 1984. She has helped to make two films, *Awake from Mourning* and *Tsiamelo: A Place of Goodness*, both of which have had international distribution. Her best-selling autobiography, *Call me Woman*, was published in 1985.

■ **Liseka Mda** writes: 'I was born in Umtata, a small town in the Eastern Cape, and I live in Johannesburg, where I am some kind of writer. What I write, exactly, I'm not sure. When I wrote my matric, I was planning to study computer programming, but when the results came out, my Physical Science and Mathematics grades were dismal. Meaning I couldn't do computers. I had decided it wasn't what I wanted anyway. So one of my sisters suggested I study Journalism, seeing that I was very snoopy. When I got the Journalism degree, all the newspapers in the country were retrenching staff. I had decided I did not want to write for a newspaper anyway. So I got this job as a writer on *Upbeat*, an educational magazine for teenagers. Which is where I still am. Not that I'm sure it's what I want to do.'

■ **Fatima Meer** was born in 1929. Active in politics from her high school days, she was first banned in 1954 for two years, again from 1976 for ten years. She was imprisoned in 1976 for five months. Her political involvement has been largely education- and community-based, but has included being a founding member of the Federation of South African Women, and founding and leading the Black Women's Federation until its banning in 1978. She founded and leads the Institute for Black Research, and has survived three assassination attempts.

■ **Gcina Mhlope** writes: 'I was born in Hammarsdale near Durban. I was the last born from a large family and my name, Gcina, means the last. I grew up very attached to books as friends. I was at high school in the Transkei when I started writing poems and stories in Xhosa. I started writing in English much later, when I was already in Johannesburg, using a public toilet as my study room. Most of my published works were written in that toilet.' Gcina Mhlope is an actress at the Market Theatre, Johannesburg. She has acted at the Edinburgh Festival, and toured Britain, Europe and the USA. She plays the lead in the film *A Place of Weeping* and is planning to film her own play *Have*

182

you seen Zandile? Her stories and poems have appeared in magazines and in contemporary collections of South African writing.

■ **Bernadette Mosala** was born in 1931 in Dannhauser, Natal – one of five children. It was a rural area, and before she knew what she was up to, she was herding cattle. Later she went to a Catholic boarding school, and then to the National University of Lesotho. She became a schoolteacher, and taught high school English for seventeen years. During that time she was awarded a British Council scholarship to study Theatre and Theatre in Education at the University of Newcastle-upon-Tyne, United Kingdom. Her interest in the theatre continues. She was involved in the TV production *Maids and Madams*, and has acted in radio plays as well as directed in the theatre. She is at present working on a play, on short stories, and on a novel. She is married and has three grown-up children.

■ **Maud Motanyane** was born in sub-Nigel, a mine 40 kilometres east of Johannesburg. Although she studied Library Science at the University of Zululand, her heart had always been in writing. In 1976 she took a course in journalism, and went on to work for *The Post* newspaper. She is at present a reporter and TV critic on *The Star*. She has published articles in magazines and newspapers overseas, including *The New Internationalist*. In 1983 she was chosen as one of the fellows of the World Press Institute, St Paul, Minnesota, USA, and spent several months travelling in the United States. Maud Motanyane is a member of the African Writers' Association. She is married and has two children, Palesa, a girl of 12, and Phetheho, a boy of 9.

■ **Gladys Thomas** was born in Salt River, Cape Town in 1935. She is a housewife, and lives with her family in a council house in Oceanview Township, a ghetto suburb of Cape Town. She says of her writing: 'I write for all the courageous men, women, youth and children of all the townships in South Africa, for their perseverance in our long struggle for basic human rights and dignity. I wrote my first poem when the Group Areas Act forced the removal of my community from our homes in Simonstown.' Gladys Thomas has published poems and stories in South Africa, Germany, France, Holland, Britain, Nigeria, China and the USA. She was included in the Kwanzaa Honours List of South Africa black women writers for her contribution to the fight against apartheid (Chicago, 1978), and was nominated for the Iowa International Writers' Programme in 1983.

■ **Miriam Tlali** says: 'I'd like to present my stories with a black audience in mind, and I have never really intended to write for a white audience. I don't think it's important at this point. I don't think I could have taken up writing if it was not my desire to take part in the process of change in this country.' Miriam Tlali was born in Johannesburg, went to school in Sophiatown, and studied at the University of the Witwatersrand and at the National University of Lesotho. Until recently her two novels, *Muriel at Metropolitan* (1975) and *Amandla* (1980), were banned in South Africa, although both sold out in their first editions. *Muriel at Metropolitan* has been translated into Dutch, Polish, German, Swedish and Danish. In 1984 she published *Mihloti*, a collection of stories and articles, and a collection of short stories, *Mehlala Khatamping (Imprints in the Quicksand)*, is due to be published soon. She has published short stories and articles in magazines and journals in Britain, USA, Europe, Africa, Australia and Canada. She lives with her husband in Soweto, and has two grown-up children.